SuperHERo Tales
Volume Two
A Collection of Female Superhero Stories

Edited by Rebecca Fyfe

Copyright ©2015 Melusine Muse Press

MELUSINE MUSE
Press

www.MelusineMusePress.com

Edited by Rebecca Fyfe
Cover art by Julia Stilchen

Authors of stories within this anthology retain the rights to their own stories.

All characters in this book are fictitious, and any resemblance to actual persons, living or dead, is purely coincidental.

Stories are written by authors from all over the world, and each story retains the spelling, grammar and colloquialisms from its author's country of origin.

Dedicated to girls everywhere. You are all superheroes.

Table of Contents

Foreword by Lisa McLeod 7
Ink by Rebecca Fyfe 10
    A New World 12
Pegasus by Stephen J. Mitchell 16
    Above 17
The Abacus by Mark Dennion 20
    The Reality of a Superhero 21
Tyga by Dee Harrison 25
    Choices 26
Morpha Girl by Julia Stilchen 28
    Morpha Girl to the Rescue 29
Mirage by Tinika Ross 32
    You Only Live Twice 33
Demon Huntress by Rebecca Fyfe 37
    Not an Ordinary Day 39
Leto by Bron Rauk-Mitchell 40
    The End 42
Spectrum by Jo Hart 44
    Spectrum and Captain Awesome vs. Arachnid 45
Air-Heart by Brian Norris 48

SuperHERo Tales

    Missing Memories *49*
Fire Angel by Rebecca Fyfe *53*
    Becoming a Superhero *54*
Eronia by Michaal Tucker *56*
    Rescuing Dana *57*
Llamaphilist by Mary MacFarlane *60*
    The Llama Always Works *61*
S.O.S. by Stephen J.Mitchell *65*
    Double Jeopardy *66*
Dark Sarah by Kevin Hammond *69*
    Light and Dark *69*
Warrioress by Rebecca Fyfe *73*
    An Unexpected Battle *75*
Sand Scorpion by Michael Norwitz *78*
    Gluey Gustave *79*
Divine Light by Robert Fyfe *82*
    The First Reaping *83*
Siren by Rebecca Fyfe *87*
    The Guardian *89*
Firestick by Angelica Fyfe *92*
    Drowning *95*
Warrior by Cecilia Clark *100*
    Warrior Women *101*
About the Authors & Illustrators *109*

Foreword
by Lisa McLeod

    I never wanted to play "the girl" when I was a kid. Unfortunately, I was the only girl in a family of boys. The only advantage I had was that I was the oldest by a year, and the wisdom and authority of that year allowed me to dictate how games would be played, how stories would be told, and who would play which parts. When it came to deciding who would play which characters, I steadfastly refused to play "the girl". I would not play her when "the girl" was Princess Leia and definitely not when she was Daisy Duke. "The girl" was always secondary, never central, always an object to be looked at, never the one whose eyes we look through, always needing rescue, never rescuing (even when Leia comes to "rescue" Han, she is unsuccessful and the one who really rescues all of them is Luke – and once she fails to rescue Han, she is imprisoned in a metal bikini and attached to a leash – it wasn't really all that inspiring of a role, in my mind). Taking full advantage of my year seniority, I made my youngest cousin play "the girl", and we older kids would take turns playing the more central, male characters.

    Despite my acceptance of stories with a male character focus, I never really got into superheroes until I discovered the X-Men. Finally, I felt, there were some female characters that I would be willing to play. Rogue was my favorite character, but beyond the X-Men, I was uninspired by the female characters that then populated most of the comic world. They were not there for women to identify with; they were there for men to look at. I became more and more disenchanted with the world of comic books – only occasionally venturing into it when Star Wars and Buffy the Vampire Slayer comics became more prevalent. This feeling of alienation is one of the reasons that few women identify as comic book or superhero fans. Walking into a comic book store, it becomes painfully obvious that female characters are often there to serve the male gaze.

Thankfully, this is changing, and with this change, more women and girls are venturing into the world of comics and superheroes that has traditionally made us feel so unwelcome. The success of movies like Frozen, The Hunger Games, and Divergent, while not "superhero" stories in the purest sense, are opening doors for more female-centered stories that have strong, independent characters. Makers of comics and movies are catching on to what women like me have known and yearned for all along: female characters who are powerful, central, and fun to identify with. In an article in the Atlantic, Noah Berlatsky writes, "At a moment when superheroes are becoming more popular and comics are becoming more respected, it makes sense for publishers of superhero comics to start trying to create stories for the other half of the population."

We can see this move toward courting a female audience in the new female-led superhero movies currently in the works, including Captain Marvel and Wonder Woman. Similarly, a new cartoon called, "DC Super Hero Girls" is being launched in the fall of 2015. All of these developments bode well for the next generation of girls and boys, who will be exposed to a far greater range of strong, heroic, and interesting characters of both genders.

But there is still a great deal of progress to be made toward creating parity in the representation of women and girls in the superhero genre, and anthologies, like the one you are about to read, are an important part of making strides toward greater gender equity. In this anthology, the reader will experience stories of women and girls that are diverse and complex; stories of superheroes who challenge cultural norms, as well as fight to fit in. Anthologies like this one, give readers a chance to experience stories centered on female characters that do not have to conform to a stereotypical idea of what it means to be a woman, while at the same time, these stories help to expand our ideas of what it means to be a superhero.

The superhero genre itself has always centered on telling the stories of outsiders, of the picked-on, the weaklings, and the excluded. These tales challenge the reader to identify with the outcasts of society, to see the common humanity hidden beneath outer masks and costumes. Faced with rejection by the societies they are charged with saving, superheroes learn to use and control their unique gifts, strengths, and voices, and, in doing so, elevate not only themselves, but also the societies around them. Superhero stories build empathy for the other, whether the other is different because of their skin color, species, religion, or gender, and anthologies like this one, which focus on superheroes who happen to be female, are as important for men and boys to read as they are for women and girls. Because if we are ever going to be able to achieve greater gender equity in representations of male and female characters, we must acclimate our sons, brothers, fathers, and husbands to reading stories told from a female point-of-view, just as most women are used to experiencing stories that are told from a male point-of-view.

The stories in this anthology give readers a chance to see women and girls as a part of the larger world of superheroes; as central and complex characters in their own right, rather than as secondary characters whose role is only relevant in its relationship to men. These stories are for you, whether you are a woman or man, girl or boy, and I am more excited than ever that the stories of female superheroes are finding their place alongside, rather than behind, their male counterparts. Female characters no longer have to play second fiddle to more central, male characters, and nowhere do I see this better demonstrated than when I watch my daughter happily pretend to be a strong female superhero. Nothing makes me smile more than knowing that she never feels like playing "the girl" is something derogatory, and even better, my son doesn't see it that way either. We have come a long way since I was a kid, and we've only just begun.

Ink
by Rebecca Fyfe

Name of female superhero: Ink

Name of human alter ego, if different: Jasmine Storm

Superhero appearance (hair, eyes, body type, etc.): She has completely blacked out eyes, long, straight black hair, an inky mask over her eyes and a swirling black mist around her.

Human alter ego appearance (if she has an alter ego): She has long, wavy, red hair with blonde highlights. She is petite and fit with light hazel eyes, freckles and pale skin.

Costume: When her tattoos swirl around her, they make whatever she is wearing appear black. They also create a mask over her eyes and darken her hair. Her eyes become completely black from the whites and all the way across them.

Personality: She is witty, kind, stubborn and friendly, but she's a bit shy as herself. She's much more confident when she is in superhero form.

Brief description of how she got her powers: She is born with it but doesn't realize it until she randomly begins developing her power in her early teens. As she gets older, it becomes stronger, and she starts using her powers to help others when she is in her early 20s.

Powers: She can control ink. At first, she can just control ink on the page and make it take on different shapes, but eventually she can take control of ink tattooed on her body and make the tattoos come to life for her to use and then return to her at will. Her power continues to grow and, in the future, she will be able to absorb the ink from pictures and make them into tattoos for her to use later or just immediately bring them to life. The ink absorbed this way only works for a limited time though, unlike her permanent tattoos. When it stops working for her, it returns to the
page. She has the tattooed wings on her back which enable her to fly. She has tattoos of wolves, dragons, a phoenix, a tiger, daggers and, eventually, a sword. She has a Celtic-styled tattoo on her forehead which alters itself and becomes a mask for her when she is using her powers.

Anything else important: She has a best friend named Jack. Jack is an artist and he is the one who creates her tattoos for her. He helps

her develop her powers and, when she starts being able to absorb ink from a page, he starts sketching special weapons which she can use. The world she lives in is one full of supernatural creatures, many of whom are threats to humanity. There is an organization called PITS which wants to register all Paranormals, and there is also a hate group of Normals which wants all Paranormals locked up or killed, so it is imperative that she keeps
her identity a secret.

A New World

    The ink from the dagger tattooed into my forearm swirled into a misty black smoke and reformed whole in my hand.
    "Still want a piece of me?" I challenged the two guys who had groped me and pulled me into the alley as I passed.
    I held the dagger like a pro. It was clear I knew how to use it. Black ink from the many tattoos I sported coalesced into dark, inky smoke which surrounded me, weaving through my hair, changing it from dark red to inky black. More of it swirled around my waist. Different shapes could be seen periodically in the black mist surrounding me, shapes of dragons and tigers and more, but none of it fully took form.
    One of the tattoos on my face oozed and spun, changing shape, reforming into a dark mask over my eyes. Some of the tattoo ink covered my irises and the whites of my eyes. I knew it made my eyes look completely, demonically black.
    Both men put their hands up in placating gestures. "We just wanted a little fun. No harm meant. Honest!" The taller of the two tried to placate me.
    "We'll just leave you alone now. We didn't mean nothin' by it. A'right, miss?" said the other as the two of them began backing away cautiously.
    I knew I appeared fierce and fearless in my stance and in my anger, but the truth was, I had been momentarily panicked when they had grabbed me. Old fears had wedged, momentarily, in my heart, and that moment of pure fear only made me even angrier now. It took all of my will to let the two creeps go, when everything in me

wanted to strike out at them, wanted to make them feel fear, but I reigned in that need for retaliation and stood motionless as they left.

Once they were gone, the inky mist surrounding me dissipated and my tattoos reappeared on my body, back where they belonged. My eyes returned to their usual light hazel and my hair returned to its natural dark red with blonde highlights. My skin was still pale and freckled, but I'd never been able to change anything about that, even with my tattoos and my supernatural gift of controlling them.

I left the alley and continued on my journey as if nothing had happened.

I hadn't always had this gift. But it served me well in the altered world in which I now lived.

Almost exactly a year had passed when the world had learned that all of those things that went bump in the night and the monsters they feared in their nightmares were actually real. The Paranormal Institute for Temporal Studies, or PITS as it was known, had broadcast a live video over many of the main network television stations of a young man, no more than twenty or so years old, transforming into a massive wolf. The transformation had been gruesome and bloody, and the man had been in so much obvious pain that it had been painful to watch. But nevertheless, millions had watched that first televised transformation of an actual werewolf and, from that point on, the world had become something new.

It had come to light, since then, that vampires were real and that ghosts actually existed. Everyone was left wondering, if werewolves, vampires and ghosts were real, what else was out there that we didn't know about? No one had any evidence yet that things like fairies, mermaids, unicorns, trolls and other creatures from mythology were real, but who was to say they weren't, now that other mythical creatures had been proven to be real?

A new task force had been formed immediately with the purpose of registering all Paranormals and policing their activities. And, as happened with any other group found to be different, groups of "Normals" had formed hate groups. Hate groups seemed to crop up for all sorts of reasons, but the main reason was usually fear, and what was more fear-inducing than the monsters of your horror stories coming to life?

The government hadn't discovered any other Paranormals though – just the ones that PITS had already proven existed. But I knew there were other types of Paranormals out there. I'd always thought I was one of the Normals, until my early teen years, when strange things had started happening around me.

It had started with a sketch. I'd been looking at a sketch, thinking that it was lovely but that the hand looked unnatural. That's when the ink that made up the hand in the sketch started to move on the page, changing the hand on the sketched woman into something that looked much more like a hand to me than the one the sketch had started with. I thought I had imagined it.

But it didn't end there. Little by little, I started having more control over ink. I could manipulate ink on a page to look any way I wanted it to look. After playing with this for a while, I started wondering about tattoos and if the ink would react to me the same way in the form of a tattoo as it did on the page.

My first tattoo was the dagger on my wrist. When I learned that I could make that tattoo leave my body and reform as a real dagger, I started experimenting with more complicated ideas. I have two dragon tattoos and a tiger tattoo, all of which I can bring into being with nothing more than a thought and my own will to make it so. I have another dagger tattooed on one of my calves, and I have a Celtic symbol tattooed on my forehead that becomes my mask when I need it.

The tattoo I am most proud of though is the tattoo of wings across my back. With them, when I bring them into being, I can actually fly. I haven't managed much control in the air yet, but, I figure, it's a learning process.

The mask was my friend Jack's idea. He's an artist. He works at a tattoo parlor to pay for his tuition at the local university. He's the one who created all of my tattoos. And he's the only one who knows about my special gifts. He knew how much I wanted to use my new-found power to help others, so he came up with the tattoo being used as a mask in order for me to hide my identity whenever I help someone.

PITS, which is the organization that the government repurposed to patrol the Paranormals, isn't very good at its job. Now that they no longer have to hide who they are, Paranormals have more time to do the things that they do best. For vampires, that means they are killing more people. It's not official or anything, but everyone knows that most of the disappearances in the main part of the city are vampire-related. Werewolves mostly stick to the suburbs or the countryside. People do get hurt by them from time to time, but it's not as much of a problem as the vampires are becoming.

Of course, we don't yet know what else is out there. When I think about how many fairy tale creatures like the taste of human meat, I become very scared for humanity. I like to think that it's why my powers showed up when they did, so I can do something about it, so I can help save people. Maybe it's so I can help even up the odds between Normals and Paranormals.

Yah, okay; I'm not exactly a Normal anymore. But PITS doesn't know that, and as long as they don't know about me, I can do some good. Besides, how can they register me when I don't think there is even a name for what I am?

In the meantime, the Paranormals that lurk in the shadows, waiting to hurt others, had better watch their backs, because I'll be coming for them.

Pegasus
by Stephen J. Mitchell

Name of female superhero: Pegasus

Name of human alter ego, if different: Princess Solaria

Superhero appearance (hair, eyes, body type, etc.): She has a light blue skin tone with golden hair and wings. She also has a golden horn that shimmers, extends and retracts from her forehead at will.

Human alter ego appearance (if she has an alter ego): She doesn't have one; she lacks the ability to blend in with the human race.

Costume: She wears a white tunic and skirt. The sun (her royal family crest) is embroidered over her left breast.

Personality: She is arrogant and playful.

Brief description of how she got her powers: Her powers are fueled by magic that is not of this world.

Powers: She is endowed with extraordinary strength and the ability to fly. She uses magic to break the laws of nature set by this realm.

Anything else: As with all royalty from her realm, she is bound to protect the innocent until she is deemed worthy to sit upon the throne.

Above

    The car speeds through the city streets with reckless abandon. The man behind the wheel has just committed a heinous crime and is hoping to escape. Panic hasn't served him well; unfortunately the fear of being caught has drawn plenty of attention to his plight. Taking advantage of the fact that local law enforcement try to pursue him while taking innocent bystanders into account, he is able to put some space between himself and the police.
    That's where I come in.
    Running along the rooftops, parallel to his escape route on the streets below, I track his every move. When I see him swerve to avoid a car caught in the intersection, I leap down with my arms outstretched. As I plummet to the street below, I wait for just the right moment before unfurling my beautiful wings to catch an updraft and glide effortlessly towards the fleeing criminal.
    He finds some open road as he moves further away from the city and accelerates, allowing him to outrun me, only for the moment. I bring my arms in tight to my body and give one powerful flap of my wings, and I'm suddenly closer than I was before. The car gives a jolt, and he almost loses control of it.
    He sees me now.
    Like an eagle toying with its prey, I continue to let him enjoy his moment by weaving in and out of his view. He's reached the on-ramp now and intends to get on the highway. Good, now I can really show off what my wings can do. Flapping with renewed vigor, I

easily outpace him and look over my shoulder as he is now behind me. Twisting my body, I stop in midflight to face him with my wings outstretched. The car comes screeching to a halt as he fusses about for his sidearm.

"Leave me alone, you flying freak!" He aims his gun at me and pulls back on the hammer to arm its chamber. The first time someone aimed a gun at me, I was terrified. I had heard of weapons similar to these used to hunt down and kill my people.

"Shoot me, if you please," I tell him. "It will make no difference as to how your day ends."

He fires his gun. Again, I tease by dodging each round as it pierces the air. To me, it all appears to move in slow motion as my reflexes are beyond this realm. Having full control over my limbs and wings, I guide them around each bullet until the last one reaches me. That one I catch in my chest and my wings wrap around my body as I fall to the ground.

Curled up in a ball, I lay still. My breathing sputters out as my heart rate slows to a crawl. It's dark. My wings encapsulate me but as my body relaxes, they unfurl, exposing me to what once was my prey. I hear his footsteps approach as he reloads his weapon. Standing above me, aiming for my head, I hear the last words he'll ever speak to me, "Time to die, you weirdo freak of nature."

Smiling, I open my hand to reveal the last bullet – the one I caught. His jaw drops as I leap up from the ground. Spinning in the air like a whirlwind, I knock the gun from his hand. With both hands, I grip his dirty leather jacket and hold him still as my deadly, but beautiful, horn rises from my forehead to a sharp point, stopping a hair's width from his neck. Stricken with fear, as most of these humans are when confronting their own mortality, his eyes widen.

"Put him down!" My attention is drawn by a force of police cars. They must've arrived during my moment of arrogance. "I repeat, set the man down and surrender yourself to us."

They hate me, in spite of all I do for them to keep this world safe, bound by my royal heritage to do so. I do not belong here, but as any who long to someday sit on the throne of my home world, I must prove myself worthy first. They all point their guns at me, regardless of the good I do for them. I've been here for five Earth years now, and still, they treat me like a freak of nature. I'd just as soon leave them to continue destroying themselves, but, alas, I cannot.

They are a fragile race and have not yet learned acceptance of one another. Instead, they preach tolerance, which only buries their hatred for each other under a facade of togetherness.

With a swift motion, I throw the criminal towards the barricade of police cars. His leather protects him as he slides on the pavement to a halt. I jump into the air, and all it takes is one powerful, majestic flap of my beautiful wings to knock them all to the ground as I soar high into the air.

They will someday understand that I'm here to help them. And at the same time, learn that I am above them.

The Abacus
by Mark Dennion

Name of female superhero: The Abacus

Name of human alter ego, if different: Abigail "Abby" Cust

Superhero appearance (hair, eyes, body type, etc.): Abacus has a small, lithe body that is not overly physically powerful. She has never really felt that much of a need to do much physical exercise; she sees it more as a way to pass the time than to look better. Most of her face is covered by a ski mask, but her grey eyes are visible. She is 5'2" without her boots on.

Human alter ego appearance (if she has an alter ego): Abigail is not a trendy girl. She likes to wear what she finds comfortable and appealing without caring what others may think. Most of the time, she can be seen wearing t-shirts of her favorite superheroes because she is such a huge comic fan. Abby has raven black hair with a red fringe at the end. She is often seen wearing her Music World employee badge lanyard around her neck.

Costume: The Abacus constructed her own costume from items she found in her house. She wears a navy blue ski mask over her face. Her feet are protected by a normal pair of Timberland hiking boots. On her hands, she wears brown gardening gloves that looked like they could have come from any home improvement store. Finally, she wears a yellow leotard with a calculator pad sewn onto it.

Personality: Abigail is her own person. When growing up, she found that math was extremely easy for her, but reading was always difficult. This difficulty led her to find comic books which started her life-long infatuation with superheroes. This attribute, compounded with the fact that she was a girl doing extremely well in a subject that girls are often told they can't succeed in, has caused Abby to create a "who-cares" attitude to what others think of her. Conversely, The Abacus feels that she is almost invincible. She is willing to put herself into any life-threatening situation, for nothing less than just to banter with the villain.

Brief description of how she got her powers: The Abacus was born with her powers.

Powers: The Abacus has one true superpower – she is phenomenal at math. Complex equations and calculus problems entertain her as much as a book would entertain a normal person. In addition to this, a life-time study in superheroes has made her exceptional in other traditional hero traits such as banter and catch phrases.

Anything else important: Abby Cust grew up with the idea that superheroes were synonymous with fairy tales – they were just fiction. Then one day, a group of super-powered people, the Human Dictionary, Atlas and a talking dinosaur named Thesaurus Rex, showed up in her home town and start taking down a local street gang known as the Wu Slang Clan. With the idea that superheroes are real, she sets out to find her inner superhero, and tries to take on a member of the Clan on her own.

The Reality of a Superhero

Superheroes are real! She knew this now. A life-long dream nearly come true. No longer would she have to sit in the dark and read comic books by flashlight to get her meta-human fix. No. Now, Abby Cust only had to read the headlines of the local papers for that.

But this was a dream that was *nearly* true. For as much as she loved that superheroes were real, what would make this a true fairy tale would be if she herself were a heroine! How could that be? In comics, there were five types of heroes: mutants, aliens, science or technology powered, magic users, and normal people who were well trained.

To her knowledge, she was not an alien, mutant or a sorcerer. There was always the hope that she could be fortunate enough to be hit with toxic waste or radiation, but how did she determine the amount of exposure between powers and death? But there was still the training.

Most superheroes trained themselves into incredible physical shape. That would take too long, so that idea faded too. But then she realized that there were those select heroes – the ones who trained their brains instead of their bodies. They were rare, but they were superheroes! She could do that.

For as long as she could remember, she had always been good at math – like scary good. In grade school, teachers often congratulated her for doing so well because girls weren't normally good at math. This was the motivation – the identity – that she needed. She had been a superhero her whole life, but she never knew it!

Abby Cust would buck the trend of a masculine-centered world and show all the girls of the world that not only could girls be good at math, but they could be superheroes too! She would hide her secret identity in plain sight and call herself the Abacus!

Standing on a rooftop, the Abacus stared down at one of the most dangerous alleys in the city, dressed in her home-made costume – a yellow leotard that showed off her curves (or lack thereof) with a few ironed-on patches that represented numbers. A pair of standard gardening gloves (available at any home improvement store), a blue ski mask, and a pair of size seven Timberland boots, completed her outfit.

She understood that the costume looked campy. For starters, the emblem misrepresented her as more of a calculator than an abacus, but a symbol for an abacus would look confusing. Also, she realized that better costumes were available on-line, but that could take weeks! She wanted – she needed – to be a super heroine as soon as possible. That is how she found herself on this rooftop staring down at the alley below.

For weeks, Abby had tracked the adventures of new superheroes in town – Atlas and the Human Dictionary. The heroes had apparently had a number of encounters with a local karate-fighting, slang-speaking gang known at the Wu Slang Clan – a group notoriously known for breaking any rule possible. They were all criminals, all of them. And that was why the Abacus tracked one to this very alley and watched him as he hid behind the alley dumpster.

"I hope you're enjoying yourself," she spoke to the criminal below but only loud enough for her to hear, "because your number is up!"

That was the first part of her super heroine transformation. It wasn't the costume, or even the name, but the cliché catch phrases, each one math based.

Suddenly, the screaming silence of the alley was broken by laughter. The Abacus looked across the street and watched as a middle-aged couple left the movie theater and were walking with their young son toward the alley.

"It really was a funny movie!" the father said.

The Abacus looked down into the alley way. She could see the criminal, bathed in the dim light of a broken street light, blinking at the end of the alley. In the strobe, she could easily recognize a gun gripped in the criminal's left hand.

"Come on, guys, we parked on the other side of this building. We'll save fifteen minutes by cutting through this alley," the dad spoke.

That finalized it. This family was walking straight into a trap, and only she, the Abacus, could save them. A ratio of three-to-one played in the family's favor, but the independent variable of the gun changed everything.

She thought back to every comic book that she had ever read. In these situations, the heroes either assaulted the villain, or they used a weapon to disarm them. In her haste to become a hero, Abby neglected to learn how to fight or to attain a weapon. For the first time, she thought that being a hero was too much, and that she wasn't cut out for it. Then she saw the brick.

She picked up the projectile and felt its weight. She estimated it to weigh roughly three and a half pounds, and that the wind was traveling at a mere five mph. The Abacus re-adjusted her position on the roof by a few feet.

Looking back, she saw that the family was at the mouth of the alley. It was do or die time! She released the brick, hoping that her calculations were correct. For a long moment, silence lingered. Abby worried that she had failed. Then a wet thud followed by a moan of pain confirmed a direct hit. The gang member fell to the ground at the feet of the family. His gun skittered away.

The woman screamed out of fright and grabbed her son. "Bruce! Bruce, are you alright? Thomas, check on that man!" she shouted.

The Abacus looked down from her perch on the building, satisfied. For a moment, she thought about introducing herself, but true heroes weren't in it for the credit. She looked at the alley and the family no longer in harm's way and said aloud, "Make every day count!" Then she disappeared.

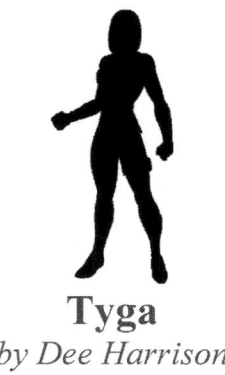

Tyga
by Dee Harrison

Name of female superhero: Tyga

Name of human alter ego, if different: Casey Aasha Lewis

Superhero appearance (hair, eyes, body type, etc.): She looks like an upright tiger with green eyes.

Human alter ego appearance (if she has an alter ego): She is a sixteen year old half-Asian, half-western girl. She is about 5' 8" tall with long, dark brown hair with an auburn streak at the front. She has green eyes and a cat-shaped birthmark on her left shoulder.

Costume: She has no costume as such, just her fur, but wears a golden gadget belt and a gold cat pendent.

Personality: She is a passionate environmentalist but has a good sense of humour and likes "fun" stuff too. She was deeply affected by her parent's deaths when she was five. She was brought up by her aunt who is Indian. She enjoys joint Western and Asian food and culture.

Brief description of how she got her powers: She was born with the potential but has to make a choice whether or not to accept them on her sixteenth birthday.

Powers: She has cat-like abilities to run, jump and leap about, along with extra good hearing and eyesight. Her fur can take on the background colours of anywhere (camouflage) and she has retractable claws.

Anything else important: She is still at college. She wants to become an environmentalist like her parents.

Choices

Aunt Sumita knelt beside her in the shrine. The towering golden statue of the Cat Goddess stared down at her; sublimely calm and yet poised on the knife-edge of violence.

"You have a choice, Casey, and you must make it honestly and without fear," said her aunt. "Accept what you are, the instincts and abilities that are within your blood and bones, and the responsibilities that come with them, or deny that part of yourself and pass the choice to the girl children you might one day have."

Casey looked down at her hands. They trembled but she could not decide if it was from fear or exhilaration. She was torn between her heart and her oh-so-sensible head. Was this the answer to her prayers, or the start of a nightmare? She tried to imagine her gentle mother kneeling in this very place, being offered the same choice. Did Mom claim her heritage? Casey did not know, and the freak accident in the rain forest that ended her parents' lives prevented her from ever knowing. All Casey wanted was to make a difference, to work hard and study to become an environmentalist like her parents. Would this help or hinder her?

"I – I need to understand more," she said quietly. "What good would it do to have these powers? How would being a Tyga make the world a safer place? Was Mom a Tyga too? 'Cos, if she was, it didn't save her or Dad when it really mattered!" Casey could not keep the sudden anger or accusation from her voice.

Sumita sighed.

"I can't tell you that, Casey," she said. "With or without the powers of your Tyga birthright, only you can desire to make a difference or not. Special abilities won't change your heart or your spirit. If you value justice, freedom and defending the defenceless, then you will pursue that regardless of anything else. I'll not lie to you. If you choose to accept this path, you will make enemies, and ruthless ones at that. Wherever the earth and its creatures are seen purely as sources of profit for exploitation by the greedy, then those enemies will oppose you and all that you stand for. But," she turned and stroked her hand through Casey's long hair, "you would not stand alone. The Tyga is the beacon, the leader of the pack, the voice of the voiceless but *she is not alone*. Your Mom found your Dad, and they worked together to build an alliance that protects this forest from the loggers and poachers."

Casey looked back up into the Cat Goddess' eyes and made her choice.

"I would not be my mother's daughter if I did not use every means at my disposal to carry on her work. I, Casey Lewis, claim my birthright. I *will* be the Tyga, and I will become the claw of the Goddess!"

Somewhere out of sight, the boom of an immense gong reverberated through the shrine.

"Then come with me and learn what you must learn," said her aunt.

Morpha Girl
by Julia Stilchen

Name of female superhero: Morpha Girl

Name of human alter ego, if different: Morley Macey

Superhero appearance (hair, eyes, body type, etc.): She has dark brown hair and gray eyes, and she is slim.

Human alter ego appearance (if she has an alter ego): She has blue hair and gray eyes, and she is slim.

Costume: She wears a blue bionic (sci-fi) super girl costume with a jet pack that allows her to fly and ejects butterfly-type mechanical wings.

Personality: She is energetic, friendly and caring. She loves to solve problems, and she's adventurous.

Brief description of how she got her powers: She was born with her powers.

Powers: Her powers are super strength, super speed and a ninja-type dexterity.

Anything else important: Nothing at this time.

Morpha Girl to the Rescue

Morley threw her covers off. The crying wouldn't stop. She could hear the wailing through the walls. She jumped out of bed and quickly dressed in her super girl outfit.

The digits on her watch flashed eight-forty.

She tucked some of her blue hair behind her ears so she could see well through her night vision goggles. She thumbed over a button on the side and pressed it. Everything changed to monochromatic green.

With one foot out before the other, she climbed out her bedroom window. Glittering lights glowed from her shoes, reflecting against the tiled roof. She crept low, edging her way along until she reached a corner. The area was clear – no eminent foes detected.

"Wings activate," she said as she pressed a button on her belt.

Two blue wings extended outward from the sides of her jet pack. She leaped into the air, gliding around a palm tree. As soon as her feet reached the green surface, she darted behind a bush.

She peeked her head around the leaves to double scan the yard. A figure hummed from the kitchen window; Momma was washing a bottle in the sink. On the second floor, Andy, her brother, was busy picking his nose near the window. First floor, Daddy sat in the living room, sipping from his drink while watching television.

Gruff popped his head out of his doghouse. His ears shot up and he cocked his head. "Arfff." He stood on his hind legs and begged for attention.

"Shhh," said Morley, pressing a finger against her lips. "Not right now."

The bulldog whimpered. He turned around and dropped himself against his cushion. He stuck his nose in the air in a protest for being hushed.

Morley dropped and rolled across the yard, hiding within the shadows. Her watched beamed eight forty-five. Above her head dangled a rope ladder. She pulled herself up to reach her tree house headquarters. The paint was peeling off the walls. The wooden boards curved slightly at the ends.

She opened a small door to a closet space where she loved keeping some of her super girl gadgets. In the back corner sat a little box. Inside was a blue, glowing crystal. She placed it into a socket on her belt.

"Beep, beep, beep." Her watched beamed eight-fifty. She hustled back down the rope ladder.

She pressed a few buttons on her wristband. The jet pack powered up in a low hum, lifting her off the ground. She zipped back over to her bedroom window and entered her room.

The crying had become louder. She darted to her door and peeked out with one eye.

"I'm com'in, sweetie pie." Momma held a bottle in her hand and entered Sarah's room. The crying decreased and, eventually, it was silent again.

Morely sighed. "Guess I won't be need'in this after all." She held up the glowing crystal.

She heard Momma's footsteps down the hall. Morley dived under her covers. The door to her room creaked open and then shut. The footsteps continued downstairs.

Cries began to stir once more. Morley got out from her bed. She tiptoed out her room and went down the hall. On her right, Sarah's door was cracked open. She let herself through and tiptoed closer to the wails.

She brought her hands over her ears, wincing as the cries vibrated near the crib.

She swung a foot up in a winged horse kick. With her toe, she turned the light switch off. The room faded into dark, slightly lit by the moonlight peering through the room window. Her watch lit up with eight fifty-five.

"It's me, Morpha Girl to the rescue!" She peered over the crib and held out the blue crystal. "I've brought you something that helped me sleep better when I was little like you." Morley placed the ball in an open slot of a device sitting on the nightstand. With a few twists of the sphere, it shot out beams of light. Starry shapes filled the room.

Morley looked over the crib and stared down at her baby sister. Her lips stretched into a smile as Sarah giggled and cooed. She glanced up at the night lights dancing around the room, glowing in colors of green, blue, red, yellow and orange.

Morley tiptoed out of the room and headed back to her bedroom.

The digits eight fifty-nine flashed. She slipped out of her Morpha butterfly, super girl suit and into her pajamas.

Nine pm.

She grabbed the end post of her bed, lifted her feet in the air into a back flip, and landed against the mattress. She crawled under the covers and leaned into her soft pillow.

"Another Supa-girl's quest completed!"

Mirage
by Tinika Ross

Name of female superhero: Mirage

Name of human alter ego, if different: Lisa Stark/Lisa Carter

Superhero appearance (hair, eyes, body type, etc): She has dark brown hair and brown eyes that can be seen through her masquerade mask. She is petite but athletic.

Human alter ego appearance (if she has an alter ego): She has medium length, dark brown hair and brown eyes. She is petite. She usually wears jeans and a t-shirt when she's not working as a police officer. When she's working, she wears a cop uniform.

Costume: She wears black combats boots, camo pants, a black tank top and a black masquerade mask.

Personality: She is good natured, intelligent and funny. She is also slightly absent-minded and sweet, but she has a temper.

Brief description of how she got her powers: She was murdered and given a second chance at life by becoming a superhero.

Powers: She has the powers of telekinesis, mind reading, levitation and the ability to walk through solid surfaces such as doors, walls, etc.

Anything else important: Lisa has to assume a new identity once she agrees to become a superhero. The new identity she assumes is a cop, which allows her to track down villains and find her murderer. Her partner, David Brooks, is the only one who knows her secret.

You Only Live Twice

Lisa yawned as she stopped for the traffic light. She was tempted to blow it. After all, there weren't a lot of people on the road at 3:00am. But it was still illegal, and as a police officer, she had no business breaking the law.

Suddenly, the light flickered. Lisa looked around at the buildings and streetlights. All the lights were going berserk until they died and darkness swept across the city. Lisa cursed, turned around and headed for the power plant.

A cold chill ran through Lisa's spine as she pulled up to the plant. Something was wrong. Normally the plant's backup generator would kick in once the power went out, but there were no lights or sounds coming from the plant.

Lisa left her car by the gate and walked towards the plant. She didn't see anything unusual until she got closer to the building. There were three unauthorized vehicles parked by the power plant's company vans. Three people scaled the towers, armed with cans and guns. She wasn't close enough to see what was happening inside of the building, but it didn't look good.

Lisa called her partner, Brooks.

"Hello?" Brooks yawned.

"Brooks – it's Lisa."

"What do you want, girl? It's – I don't even know what time it is. The power's off."

"Exactly! Something's going down at the plant."

"How do you know?" Brooks asked.

"I'm outside! There's at least three unauthorized cars here and people with guns and God knows what else. Can you check the plates for me?"

"If the station's generator is working. Rattle 'em off to me." Brooks replied.

Lisa gave Brooks the license plate numbers.

He sighed. "Got it."

"I'm going to stay here and run some recon." Lisa said.

"Don't you dare! There are at least three of them and only one of you. Wait for backup before you get killed," Brooks growled.

Lisa laughed. "It'll be fine. I'm not going to go in guns blazing. I'm just going to poke around."

"Don't! I'm serious. You don't know what they're capable of."

"You're such a worrier. I'll be fine."

"Lisa, promise you won't go in there. Stay put."

"But –"

"Stay put."

Lisa sighed. "Fine."

"Promise?"

"Promise."

"Good. Just stay where you are and keep an eye on things. I'll call you once I know who these people are and what their game is. In the meantime, I'm sending backup."

"Okay."

"And Lisa?"

"Yeah?"

"Remember, you promised."

Lisa sighed and turned her attention back to the intruders. They were climbing down from the towers. The cans turned out to be spray paint. In bold, sloppy letters they painted POWER FOR ALL. Lisa rolled her eyes. If she was going to get inside the plant, now was the time.

Lisa felt guilty for breaking her promise to Brooks. After all, he was her partner and her best friend. However, the sooner she knew what the intruders were up to, the sooner she could stop it. Besides, it wouldn't be Lisa sneaking into the plant. It would be Mirage.

Lisa hid behind the van to change into her disguise: camo pants, combat boots, black tank top and black mask. Lisa counted five intruders as they went inside the plant and barricaded themselves inside. Once the coast was clear, she pressed her hands against the wall and concentrated. The wall became fluid and rippled. Lisa walked through it and was inside the plant.

Lisa cleared her throat. "Put down your guns, boys."

The intruders looked at Lisa in shock. One of the men laughed as they pointed their guns at her. "What are you going to do if we don't?"

Lisa smiled. "This."

Their guns flew from their hands and pointed back at them. As their guns floated in the air, the triggers twitched.

"Have I made my point?" Lisa asked.

She heard the safety of another gun click from behind her. She felt the barrel on her head. "Yes, but have I?" another intruder sneered.

Lisa nodded.

"Good. Now drop the guns before you get hurt."

Lisa smiled. "I won't."

Lisa's body dropped through the floor and resurfaced behind the gunman. She punched him in the neck and he fell to the ground. A few of the other intruders grabbed their guns while she was distracted. Bullets flew through the air. Lisa ducked and dodged the bullets as best she could, but one hit her in the arm. She howled in pain. She had to get out of there.

Sirens blared as dozens of cops swarmed inside. The number of bullets in the air doubled. Another one hit Lisa. She cursed under her breath as she made her way to the rooftop and collapsed. Lisa took her hand and pressed it against one of her wounds.

"How careless you are," a man sneered from the shadows. He stepped into the light so she could see his face. Half of it was the face of a strikingly handsome Native American. The other half was an exposed skull.

"I didn't think it would be so bad. I thought I could handle it." Lisa explained.

"You didn't think! That's the problem!" he shouted.

"Phantom, I'm sorry."

"You're apology means nothing. Look at you! Bloody and broken. This is not a video game! You may have gotten a second chance at life, but that's all. If you die before you complete your mission, that's it! This will have all been for nothing."

Lisa bowed her head. The Phantom was right. Lisa had been careless with her life. She was lucky to have survived. Somewhere along the way, she forgot she was given a second chance for a reason. Her primary objective was to find out who killed her, not pretend she was in a Clint Eastwood movie.

The Phantom smiled gently at her as he helped her up. "Come on. Let's attend to those wounds so your partner doesn't know you're a liar."

Lisa frowned causing The Phantom to laugh.

SuperHERo Tales

Demon Huntress
by Rebecca Fyfe

Name of female superhero: Demon Huntress

Name of human alter ego, if different: Nicole McKay

Superhero appearance (hair, eyes, body type, etc.): She has long, black hair, usually worn in a ponytail but not always. She wears all black leather and a thin, black mask across her eyes. Her dark eyes are visible through her eye mask.

Human alter ego appearance (if she has an alter ego): She has long, brown hair, brown eyes and she's tan. She's petite but very fit.

Costume: She wears form-fitting black leather and a thin, black mask across her eyes. She carries two swords.

Personality: She is a loner. She protects the weak out of a sense of duty. She is passionate but keeps to herself because she believes that anyone who gets close to her will be endangered by the creatures she hunts.

Brief description of how she got her powers: She was born to hunt demons. The ability runs in her family, and she was trained from a very young age by her uncle.

Powers: She is fast, strong and well-trained. She heals faster than normal people, and she has a high pain tolerance.

Anything else important: She was trained by her uncle because her family was killed when she was four years old. Her uncle took her in and trained her to hunt demons, because that is what her family had always done. It is part of their heritage and why they have the abilities they have. She carries a lot of anger and mistrust inside her and she tries very hard to keep everyone at an emotional distance. She has not yet found the demon that killed her parents, but she still searches for it.

During one of her battles, she rescues a middle-aged woman named Ellie who works in an office as a programmer. They encounter each other more than once and, eventually, Ellie begins to assist her in her quest to rid the world of demons by helping with research and creating useful gadgets for her to use while in battle.

Not an Ordinary Day

I'd been working here for over thirty years and I had never seen anything like this. Even all the craziness that being a grandmother of seventeen children entails never prepared me for what was happening now. I was the last one at the office at the end of the workday.

The petite, exotic-looking girl had entered in a whirlwind of motion through the broken glass of the window that the creature had burst through. The golden-scaled creature had wings and was massive in size. The girl dove through the window following after the beast. Encased entirely in black leather, with a thin black mask over eyes, she wielded a combination of short swords, one in each hand, as if she had been born to use them.

The beast shrieked, a strange bird-like sound, as it swiped its massive claws her way, but the girl never even flinched. She cut the beast over and over as she dove and parried, narrowly missing being hurt by the beast's snapping teeth or long claws. The beast had a tail, a thick, muscular thing, which it swung at her. The force of the blow threw her across the room and into the wall with a power that shook the building, but she stood back up, hurt but still able to fight.

Stunned, I stood frozen in place, watching the battle unfold before my eyes. The beast drew blood from the girl with one quick slash of its claws. She spun, knelt and then plunged her right sword up into the creature's head through the fleshy part of its throat. The creature burst into glittery sparkles that shimmered in the air for a moment before slowly fading away.

She nodded to me, this petite warrior, and wandered out the door, and at last I was able to move. I picked up my car keys. I looked at the carnage of the office behind me, the broken desks and overturned chairs, the broken glass that covered the floor; if it weren't for that, I could assure myself that none of it had really happened.

I finished locking up and headed home. I had a late dinner to prepare for my husband. For now, my life would carry on as usual, but I had the feeling that I would be seeing this dragon-slaying girl again.

Leto
by Bron Rauk-Mitchell

Name of female superhero: Leto (in honour of the mother of Artemis)

Name of human alter ego, if different: Prior to her rebirth, our heroine's name was Kate. After her rebirth, she forms a new identity and chooses the name Diana Hunt.

Superhero appearance (hair, eyes, body type, etc.): She has waist length auburn hair with a silver streak, worn in a simple plait or braid, and piercing blue eyes. Her skin has honeyed tones. Leto has the body of a well-trained athlete. At this stage, Leto is 5'6" but she hasn't finished growing yet.

Human alter ego appearance (if she has an alter ego): Diana wears reading glasses, not out of need but as the only nod to her former life (Kate was short-sighted and wore glasses and/or contacts, but after her rebirth, her vision was 20-20). Diana occasionally wears her hair down but prefers to wear her hair up in a bun or in a silver snood. The silver streak that is a distinctive part of her superhero persona is unnoticeable while she is Diana. Diana prefers casual, almost sporty clothing or jeans and a tee.

Costume: Leto favours simple sports tunics (black, grey or dark green), with sports shorts underneath them and runners. Occasionally, she will wear a military-style garb of combat boots, tee and cargo pants. Like Celestial Arrow, Leto wears an eye mask.

Where most of her clothing is dark or in muted colours, her eye masks tend towards more showy colours to match the ribbons that she weaves through her hair.

Personality: Diana is primarily withdrawn, sullen and suspicious. She is a voracious reader and highly intelligent. She prefers the company of animals, and soon finds herself the human companion to a black stray cat, whom she calls Luna. Diana is prone to night terrors and periods of selective mutism. Diana is happiest when visiting the training camp run by Artemis. Her relationship with Phoebe is that of a younger sister; she alternates between clinginess and fierce independence. Memories of the night that she was discovered by Celestial Arrow have been suppressed, but, occasionally, flashes resurface leaving her immobilized by fear. She is energetic and eager to learn new skills.

Brief description of how she got her powers: During the worst storm to hit in decades, Celestial Arrow is prowling the city, giving assistance where needed and keeping a general eye on things, when Artemis directs her attention to a house-fire. Our young heroine, known then as Kate, has witnessed the brutal slaughter of her entire family and is close to death herself when Celestial Arrow arrives on the scene. Celestial Arrow drags her from the inferno and, with the help of Artemis, she heals Kate. They take her to the training camp run by Artemis, where she spends time healing and recuperating. Once she has regained her health and strength, Artemis offers Kate a choice: to become a Daughter of Artemis, or to start a new life with a wonderful foster family. Kate chooses to become a Daughter of Artemis. As she is a minor, she becomes a trainee and becomes the ward of Phoebe Hunt. The beasts that slaughtered Kate's family were dealt with by Artemis herself, in a manner fitting their crime.

Powers: As a trainee, Leto has been granted some powers by Artemis, and, as she matures, she will develop more of the powers belonging to Artemis. She possesses the power to call upon and communicate with animals, the ability to adopt their traits, the power of super speed, and the ability to heal herself and others (animals included). Leto's weapon of choice is a silver blow dart and she never misses her target. The darts are dipped in a strong sedative but, over time, Artemis will teach her about poisons and the darts will occasionally be dipped in these. Leto is also learning to use throwing knives. Kate was a gymnast and athlete, and Leto makes full use of these existing abilities.

Anything else important: Leto is an adolescent girl, finding her own way after the loss of her entire family. After her "rebirth" she becomes the ward of Phoebe Hunt (aka Celestial Arrow), and they live together as sisters. Leto takes a vow of chastity, at least while she is in training. The shock of losing her family sees her shun the company of most humans, preferring the company of animals, especially her cat Luna. Like Celestial Arrow, Leto will protect all that need her, especially children and animals. Leto is not Celestial Arrow's sidekick, although she will be referred to as that by those who are not in the know. She is Celestial Arrow's protégé and ward, and one day she will come into her full powers.

The End

I knew, without a doubt, that tonight I would die.
My family lay around me, all dead. My mum, my dad, and my twin baby brothers had all been senselessly and brutally slaughtered in our living room. Red, our beloved Irish setter, had valiantly given up his life, trying to protect his family. I don't know who our attackers were or how they made it into our house, nor do I know why they left me alive; all I know is that I couldn't save my family. The attackers moved swiftly, taking us all by surprise. They were methodical, brutal and without mercy. The blood-curdling screams of my baby brothers still echoed in my mind, even though they had died almost immediately. That they could kill babies without a moment's hesitation showed how inhuman our attackers were. Our screams fell upon deaf ears, and my hope was fading.
As I slipped in and out of consciousness, I could feel my life slowly ebbing away, and I knew that death was just around the corner. I felt an almost strange sense of peace, knowing that I would soon be joining my family. I didn't know what else would be waiting for me on the other side, but I was certain that my family would be there, waiting to greet me. I needed my mum to wrap her arms

around me and to tell me in her calm, soothing voice, that everything would be alright. I tried to gather some of my waning strength to crawl over to her, but, with every passing minute, I was becoming weaker.

An acrid smell slowly assaulted my nostrils. Fire! The house was on fire. I couldn't move to save my life; I would certainly die tonight. The fire was already out of control. I could hear the flames flickering nearby, and the windows began shattering around me, shards of glass embedding themselves into my savagely torn body. I was already struggling to breathe, and the smoke quickly filled my lungs, making the act of breathing torturous. I couldn't die like this; I wouldn't die like this! I tried to yell for help, but, while my lips could form the words, no sound escaped from between them.

As I began to lose my fight, the front door splintered open with a resounding crash. The silver rays of the full moon flocded the entrance and I squinted to catch a glimpse of who, or what, had shattered my front door. A gasp grudgingly escaped from between my lips. *I must be hallucinating.* I would have rubbed my eyes if it was at all possible, for standing before me was the most glorious vision. Bathed in moonlight, her white blond hair streaming around her like a silver halo, was none other than the saviour of our city, Celestial Arrow. Bending over, she quickly scooped me up, hugged me tightly to her chest, kissed my forehead and cooed reassuring sounds in my ears. I gave up my struggle, and nestled tightly against her, safe in the knowledge that I was no longer alone.

I knew, without a doubt, that I would live tonight.

Spectrum
by Jo Hart

Name of female superhero: Spectrum

Name of human alter ego, if different: Lindsay Rogers

Superhero appearance (hair, eyes, body type, etc.): She has a lean physique, dark eyes and dark hair slicked back into a ponytail.

Human alter ego appearance (if she has an alter ego): She has long, dark hair that hangs down around her face, and she wears a t-shirt, jeans and sneakers.

Costume: She wears a black bodysuit, a red utility belt and a black mask over her eyes. She completes her outfit with black boots and black gloves.

Personality: She prefers her own company. She is determined, logical, observant and intelligent.

Brief description of how she got her powers: She is born with her powers as a result of alien DNA spliced with human DNA in a government experiment.

Powers: She has super senses, an eidetic memory, and the ability to disassemble and reassemble scenes in her mind to find solutions.

Anything else important: Her super powers are also her kryptonite. When her senses are overwhelmed, she is crippled.

Spectrum and Captain Awesome vs. Arachnid

'Captain Awesome' reads the news headline on the TV.

The masked man's paunchy stomach strains against a lurid blue bodysuit and a purple cape flutters behind him. To a collective gasp from the gathered crowd, he shoots into the air and loop-the-loops against the grey sky.

Apart from flying, his only super power seems to be making media appearances. He's been on every news and talk show this week with no actual heroic deeds to his name.

The image on my TV flickers and changes. My mug slips from my hand and smashes against the tiles. Coffee pools around my feet, but I barely notice. The menacing grey-brown face on the screen has the pincer-like mouth of a spider.

"This is the Galactic Police. Earth is guilty of crimes against the galaxy and will be destroyed in one day-cycle, pending the plantation of annihilation devices at the poles."

The image flickers back to the news. The crowd's mouths hang open.

"He'll save us!" Someone points to the blue-clad superhero, whose face turns pale.

My phone vibrates. "Spectrum, get to the facility at once."

The General paces. "We messed up. We had approval to create alien-human hybrids like you, but we did some experiments we didn't have permission to conduct. We kept everything secret, but this Captain Awesome slipped under our radar."

Alien-hybrids are generally born with abilities like mine – heightened senses and a brain that disassembles and reassembles situations to see all the parts. Captain Awesome woke up several months ago hovering above his bed.

The General rubs her temples. "We're preparing a case to put before the disciplinary committee, but we need more time. I'm sending Night Falcon to the North Pole. You'll head to the South Pole with Captain Awesome. Stop this alien before he sets off the devices."

"Captain Awesome is working for you? He's just a poser."

"We need him under our supervision, and we can't hide him now that the public knows about him. Let the people think he's saving the world while you do what you have to do."

My bulky coat restricts my movements, but I'm glad for the warmth it provides me against the Antarctic air as we clamber from the helicopter.

"Where now, faithful sidekick?" Captain Awesome places his hands on his hips, taking a stance like a comic book hero.

"I'm not your sidekick," I say through gritted teeth.

My senses take over. Each distinct smell paints a picture - *the salty sea, Captain Awesome's strong body odour, penguins, fish – and there! An acrid out-of-place smell.* "That way."

Captain Awesome grabs me and takes off into the air. It's faster and easier to fly than to trek across the ice, but the close contact irks me.

A black hexagonal airship stands out against the white continent. Even Captain Awesome spots it easily.

The alien's arachnid similarities become more apparent as we near him. Though his torso resembles a human male's, he has a spider's abdomen. Four spindly legs extend from where his torso and abdomen meet and two pairs of thin humanoid arms extend from his shoulders.

"We come in peace!" Captain Awesome says as we hit the ground with a jolt.

"Be gone, human."

Awesome walks towards the alien with hands splayed and a jovial smile plastered on his face. "What has Earth done that's so bad? We're just hanging here in the Milky Way, minding our own business."

The alien snorts. "Hardly. You're proof of that."

Awesome's smile falters. "Me?"

"A human who can fly?"

"But it just happened – no one's at fault."

"You are a by-product of unapproved inter-planetary experimentation."

It takes him a minute to understand. "I'm not an alien!" He charges, red-faced.

With the alien distracted, I put my senses to work to locate the device. The acrid smell belongs to the alien, his ship has a metallic scent, but the device – I inhale deeply – an ashy smell. I estimate it's two feet under the snow on the far side of the ship. The other two are too intent in their battle to notice me slip off.

Even with my gloves and bulky jacket, the cold pierces my skin with burning intensity as I plunge my hand into the snow. The metal rod I pull out has the length and diameter of a rolling pin. It's black except for a glowing red line around the centre. On instinct, I twist it and it opens. Inside, wires criss-cross and little lights flash. I disassemble the wiring in my mind. *Thread-like black wire attached to core – probably sets the device off – don't touch it. Several thick wires – look important, but no smell or visual evidence of electrical impulses – decoys. An unobtrusive wire to the side – that's the one.* Everything reassembles. I yank out the wire. The lights stop blinking and the electrical impulses die.

Captain Awesome and the arachnid roll around on the ice – a ball of arms and legs.

"Help," Awesome grunts from the muddle.

"Just fly."

He shoots into the air, dangling the alien by one foot.

Awesome tosses me his phone. "Take a photo."

With the device and alien in the government's hands, a flock of reporters mobs us on our return.

"We saw your photo on Twitter, Captain Awesome. You're our hero!"

"I couldn't have done it without my trusty sidekick."

He sweeps his hand towards me. I freeze. Aside from my irritation at being called his sidekick, I'm mortified at being brought to the reporters' attention. I don't want any exposure. Questions fire at me and cameras flash. My ears sear with pain and my brain goes into overload from the onslaught of stimulation on my senses.

An arm wraps around me, holding me steady until I find myself in the backseat of a car. I put my head down between my knees and breathe deeply. My head clears. When I raise it again, Captain Awesome is studying me.

"Thanks."

He grins his trademark smile. "No problem. We superheroes have to stick together."

Air-Heart
by Brian Norris

Name of female super hero: Air-Heart

Name of human alter ego, if different: *Human:* Lainnie Reed. *Angel fuser:* Ariel

Superhero appearance (hair, eyes, body type, etc.): Her superhero appearance is the same as her human appearance with the exception of wings of light.

Human alter-ego appearance (if she has an alter ego): Lainnie is Native American, with straight long black hair, dark brown (almost black) almond shaped eyes, prominent cheek bones and olive skin.

Costume: She wears a gold armor breast-plate, shin, and arm guards. She wears an orange dress with tulle underlay, camouflage leggings, and brown elbow and knee pads. Air-Heart wears a red make-up mask and a brown wig.

Personality: Lainnie is very creative and passionate. She sees herself as an artist, and that is where she developed the idea for her original t-shirt designs. As an artist, she is very emotional and dramatic. She has a natural tendency to want to go against the norm, break rules and question authority.

Brief description of how she got her powers: Upon Lainnie's untimely death, she was fused with an angel whose mother was a good witch and whose father was a bad angel. Lainnie is the third human to be fused with the angel Ariel.

Powers: *Angelical:* Her angelical powers give her powers of the soul, spirit and body, which are a shield, a sword and strength, respectively.

Witch craft: Her witch powers give her the power of the four elements: water, fire, air and earth, which give her the powers of tracking, predictions, flight and incantation, respectively.

Anything else important: Lainnie Reed is a ballet student at a prestigious ballet academy in Portland, Oregon, and she designs clothes and make-up when she's not saving the world as Air-Heart.

Missing Memories

I hear voices coming towards me; they're faint, so I can't understand what they're saying. Opening my eyes, I realize I'm lying on the ground. I look up and around. I have no idea where I am –

some sort of outdoor plaza. At the top of a set of steep steps in front of me, there's a stand-alone Starbucks, and, across the street, a Nordstrom. Nothing looks familiar. Then panic sets in as I notice I'm lying in a pool of blood. I scream. I check my arms and my legs, but nothing appears broken, and I don't seem to be in any pain. I'm wearing cute skinny jeans, and a bedazzled t-shirt that reads, '*I am an artist*.' There's a large, tan tote bag next to me. Is it mine?

"What is going on?" I finally ask. My voice cracks.

"You're supposed to be dead, Lainnie," a boy says from a distance to my left. Is that my name? Am I Lainnie? I have no idea. But something tells me I don't always do what I'm supposed to.

I whip around and see a group of boys jaunting down the steps, coming my way. There's a dark skinned boy, two Asian guys, a short Latin kid, and a very tall white kid with dark wavy hair. I'm guessing they're rejects from the latest boy band, because that's exactly what they look like. I take hold of the tan bag and start to get up.

"Grab her phone," the dark boy tells the Latin kid as he points to what I'm assuming is my phone. It's too far away for me to reach.

"You idiot," the white kid says, "If you're gonna try and kill someone, you'd better make sure and do it! If she gets away, she'll tell someone!"

"Yeah, and I can't get expelled," one of the Asian guy's insists, "I'll get sent home, and my parents will definitely kill me!"

Why all this talk of killing? And why would anyone want to try and kill me?

"Well then," the dark skinned boy growls, "I guess we can't let her get away!"

Before I can move, a man swoops down in-between us. The boy band rejects stop, scream and run away. Wait – did I say a man swooped down? Yes, from the sky! Only, upon closer inspection, I realize he's about seven feet tall, wearing unbecoming, ragged clothes, has grey, burnt and blistery skin, glowing red eyes, and – has – wings! Black wings!

"So," his voice is extremely low and thunderously loud, "you have returned, Ariel." Dark smoke trails from his mouth as he talks. "And though this human you incarnated is much stronger than the last, you are foolish to think she can stop us!"

"Us?" You mean there are more? Great.

"The Sons of the Morning Star will prevail!"

There's no place I know of to run, so I just stay where I am. I'm sure I don't seem at all intimidating. "Don't be offended," I say apologetically, "but do I know you?" I'm only slightly concerned that I'm not more afraid of this winged man.

"The human does not," he responds as he walks towards me, "but the one who took over her soul does!" He reaches up, and a sword of black light appears in his right hand. "It matters not, because I will exterminate her before your memory returns!"

Without thinking, my knees bend, and I jump out of the way as the grey man slashes his sword onto the ground. It sounds like an explosion. My leg kicks up high as I execute quite an impressive split in the air. I am overcome with emotion; extreme joy floods through me. Joy? Yes, joy. Being in the air is joyous! It's as if my soul needs to fly. As soon as I'm air-born, vibrant white wings of light appear on my back. I'm actually flying! The grey man takes in a deep breath and spits black fire at me. My instinct is to put up my arms for protection, and as I do, a round shield of light appears in front of me. As the flames pass, I realize they're not hot but cold. Not the strangest thing to happen today, but I find it kind of odd.

There are buildings all around the plaza, so I decide to stay where I am. If we venture deeper into the city, someone may get hurt. Just then, my opponent flies over to me and kicks at my shield. The impact thrusts me back to the ground. "Ugh!"

Landing into the base of a column, the force causes it to tip over. As I look up, I, again instinctively, jump up and catch it before it hits the ground. At this point nothing surprises me, so I just go with it. I'm super strong. As my grey opponent lunges towards me again, I take the column and swing at him. On impact, he screams, and disappears in a burst of black flames. I set the column down and look around. Some people are watching from a safe distance, wondering what I'm gonna do next, I suppose. I run over to my bag, and rummage through it; there must be a clue inside as to who I am.

I find: leotards, tights, leg warmers, hair pins, make-up, pointe shoes, sweats, two tennis balls and a wallet! I frantically open it, and slip out what looks like ID. *West Coast Academy of Ballet. Summer Intensive. 2014. Lainnie Reed.* I pull out another card. A Tribal ID card. *Kalapuyan Tribe. Oregon.* Again, *Lainnie Reed.*

DOB: 11/04/99. There's also a debit card, a Metro Pass, and thirty bucks. Nothing about where I live. Looking at my watch, like I have somewhere to be, I find it's 6:30am. I really hope every morning doesn't start this way, because I'm already exhausted.

"Well, Academy of Ballet," I sigh, "here I come!"

SuperHERo Tales

Fire Angel
by Rebecca Fyfe

Name of female superhero: Fire Angel

Name of human alter ego, if different: Kelly Martin

Superhero appearance (hair, eyes, body type, etc.): She has long, curly red hair, usually tied up in a high and tight ponytail, freckles and green eyes. She is short, slightly plump and curvy and has large wings that are a combination of brown, orange, yellow, red and white. She wears a costume and mask.

Human alter ego appearance (if she has an alter ego): She has long, curly red hair that is usually worn down. She has freckles and green eyes. She is short, slightly plump and curvy and usually wears jeans and a t-shirt.

Costume: She wears black leather trousers which are form-fitting but not too snug, and a black leather vest-type of shirt with an open back that just has ties across it to make room for her wings. She also wears a small leather eye-mask across her eyes to help hide her identity.

Personality: She is feisty and temperamental. She tries to hide her insecurities by acting brazen. She has a soft side but tries to hide it. She is impulsive and adventurous.

Brief description of how she got her powers: In a world of superheroes and supervillains, Kelly is tired of needing to be rescued. She wants to take charge and be a hero herself. She convinces a very clever friend who studies genetics and chemistry to create a chemical that will alter her DNA.

Powers: She has wings and can fly. She has super-strength and agility, and she has faster-than-normal healing

Anything else important: Her friend Camryn is a genius when it comes to manipulating DNA and working with chemicals. Camryn is a superhero in her own right, due to her intelligence and abilities to create life-saving or life-changing concoctions. Kelly and Camryn are best friends and fiercely loyal to one another.

Becoming a Superhero

As Kelly zipped up her leather trousers, she sucked in her breath. *Whew!* It was time to stop eating so much junk food. Her trousers were getting tight. She adjusted her mask to make sure it was on straight and covered her features. She made sure to grab the leather vest that had already been altered with two long slits up the back.

"Are you sure you're ready for this?" Camryn asked, concern causing a frown line to appear above her eyes.

"Cam, I'll be fine. We've practiced my flying, and I've been training in self-defense. I'll be *better* than fine."

"But they have guns! You can't dodge bullets, Kelly, no matter how fast you've become."

"I'll just have to use the element of surprise against them. They'll be so startled when they see me, that I'll be able to take them out before they even realize what's happening." Kelly treated Camryn to her cockiest smile. "I've been training for this moment for months, Cam. If I don't do this now, I *never* will."

Cam scowled but nodded her acquiescence. "Go on then. Those hostage-takers aren't going to wait forever."

Kelly smiled and rushed out the door. When she got to the street, two very large, feathered wings burst from her back. A small grunt was all that she allowed to escape, despite the excruciating pain she felt every time her wings manifested, ripping apart her skin anew each time. Fortunately, she healed unusually fast, so the bleeding stopped and the skin knit back together around the wings within minutes. In the golden sunlight, her wings reflected golden yellow and red tones, mixed in with the white. It's why, in certain light, Camryn thought they looked like wings of fire.

Kelly's large wings stirred up a lot of wind as she took to the air, a massive smile on her face. Camryn was always a little bit jealous when she watched Kelly fly. Camryn was a complete wimp, so she'd never want to experience the pain that Kelly experienced each time she brought out her wings, but still – who wouldn't want the ability to fly?

Kelly was flying into a potentially very dangerous situation, and yet, Camryn could hear Kelly's laughter as she flew into the distance. Kelly had more bravado than the average person, and she thrilled at the idea of taking on challenges.

Those bank robbers didn't stand a chance.

Eronia
by Michael Tucker

Name of female superhero: Eronia

Name of human alter ego, if different: Jessica Haas

Superhero appearance (hair, eyes, body type, etc.): She is petite and athletic but of a realistic build. She has short chestnut hair, and is about 5'6". Her natural eye color is lavender.

Human alter ego appearance (if she has an alter ego): She dresses in standard contemporary clothing for her age group. She wears blue colored contacts to hide her eye color and a blonde wig to hide her hair.

Costume: She wears all black, light weight material (yoga pants?) with a black hoodie. Her face mask is white and featureless except for eye holes.

Personality: She is book smart and street smart, as well as strong willed. She cannot stand injustice of any kind but does not believe in the justice system. She will not kill unless absolutely necessary.

Brief description of how she got her powers: Jessica is born with her powers as a delayed result of genetic experimentation that was done on her grandmother while she was imprisoned in German concentration camps.

Powers: She has the power of extreme telekinesis, both in terms of brute force and subtle control.

Anything else important: She absolutely refuses to be owned by anyone.

Rescuing Dana

Dana was tired.

"I'm sorry, sir," she said wearily, putting on the best smile she could. "Could you repeat that, please?" She was the kind of tired that made it hard to stand, let alone think. She had already put in over twenty hours here at the coffee shop, and it was only Tuesday. Add to that the hours she had put in studying for midterms and hanging with her boyfriend, and she had not had much sleep in – what, 5 days? She had lost track.

Dana was in her second year of med school and was doing great – well, great for her, at least. She obviously had the smarts to have made it to med school, but she had been nowhere near the head of her class in high school and was even further down the food chain here. Still, she had held her own so far. However, she'd had to start working on her thesis this week (which she would have to defend next year) as well as start her third lab rotation.

Then there was Bobby, her boyfriend. He wasn't a bad guy or anything. In fact, things had been going quite well since they started dating. They had met at the college fitness center. After finishing her yoga class, she had cleaned up and had stopped at the gym store to buy a bottle of water on her way to work. He had been in line in front of her, buying some pill packs for muscle growth. Normally, she would have not given him the time of day, him being a 'meat head muscle mule,' as her father had called weight lifters. When he had started up a conversation, though, his smile and charm had won her over enough to agree to coffee.

These days, that charm was fading. He was growing increasingly unhappy with her lack of time, and as his understanding and patience decreased, his complaining increased. She tried to fit him in where she could, trying to make him happy, but that only served to cut further into what little time she had left for sleep.

So it came as no surprise to her that she had misunderstood the man standing at the counter in front of her.

"I said," he replied with a cold smile that only graced his lips, pulling a gun from his pocket, "give me all of your money."

Suddenly, Dana was quite awake. She was aware now of the details she had missed at first. The guy's skin appeared clammy, and the gun was shaking. His clothes were weeks past needing a wash, as was his hair. He was nothing like her normal clientele.

"P-Please," she stammered. "I-I don't have access to the safe. I can make deposits into it, but I can't open it. Only the manager can."

The man's smile faltered, as sweat began to form in small beads on his forehead. "Give me what's in the register then!" he snarled at her.

Dana had a rush of fear-based adrenaline that made her feel like she could run a marathon. She had just made a deposit into the safe not five minutes before the man's arrival. There was nothing in the register but the base $50 in small bills and change she was required to keep. Maybe if she was lucky... She opened the drawer to the register and was about move back when a gleam of sunlight caught her eye. Looking out the front window of the store, her heart sank. It was a police car, with two cops getting out. The would-be thief had seen it too.

He looked back at her with equal parts hatred and panic. "You stupid – you tripped some kind of alarm!!"

"No, I swear, I didn't!" She closed her eyes even as she heard the shot.

And nothing happened.

Opening her eyes with a gasp, Dana quickly looked at her chest and stomach for blood, but found none. Then she looked up to meet the equally stunned eyes of the thief. Between them, in mid-air, was the bullet. After a second more, it dropped to the floor.

"That wasn't very nice," said a small, quiet voice from the far side of the room. Both Dana and the thief quickly turned their heads to see a small woman in all black standing amidst the tables. At least, Dana *thought* it was a woman. The shape was right, but her features where hidden under a pearl white mask (featureless save two eyeholes) and her head was covered by a hood. But the eyes – they were stunning. They were the purest lavender color.

The thief spun his gun at the newcomer, firing three quick shots. Again, the bullets just stopped in the air, then dropped.

"Not too bright, are you?" the newcomer asked. "Sit down." With that, a chair slid across the room and caught the thief in the back of his knees, causing him to sit down unceremoniously. Before the thief could move, the gun was ripped from his hand and spun in the air to point at him.

"Don't be more stupid than you already have been," she warned.

Dana started as the two police officers came rushing in the front door with their guns drawn, yelling to put their hands up – until they saw the gun floating on its own. They exchanged a brief look at each other before hurtling backwards to be pinned to the wall behind them, their feet dangling.

Looking at Dana, she said with a grin, "Just like men, to come charging in half-cocked and waving their weapons at the first thing they see. You'll be fine now though."

"Nothing personal, boys," the newcomer continued as she walked towards the door. "I just can't stand around answering questions tonight – things to do. The *real* bad guy is all yours though. Ta-ta!!"

"Wait!" Dana shouted. "Who – *what* – the heck are you?"

"I'm Eronia," the newcomer replied, and vanished into the night.

Llamaphilist
by Mary MacFarlane

Name of female superhero: Llamaphilist

Name of human alter ego, if different: Lynne Schulz

Superhero appearance (hair, eyes, body type, etc.): She is a teenager. She has brown hair that hangs past her shoulder-blades in a ponytail with no bangs. She also has green eyes and a willowy frame.

Human alter ego appearance (if she has an alter ego): Her human appearance is the same as her superhero appearance, though she wears her hair more ways than just in a ponytail.

Costume: She wears a lightweight, form-fitting, lilac turtleneck with a dark purple silhouette of a llama stitched onto the chest. She also wears a dark purple bandit mask with matching dark purple gloves that go to her mid-forearm. She wears black, skinny pants tucked into knee-high dark purple boots and a dark purple belt.

Personality: She is supportive, outgoing, responsible, sassy and thoughtful. She likes resolving conflicts, and she's dependable, holistic, innovative and intelligent.

Brief description of how she got her powers: She was born with her powers which were first discovered on a field-trip to a petting zoo when she was in kindergarten.

Powers: She can communicate telepathically with llamas within a 5-10 mile radius, depending on how many trees, buildings, etc., interfere, and verbally with llamas within 5-10 feet, depending on how well the llamas feel like listening.

Anything else important: Llamaphilist often works with Lozenger (a fellow high school student who has the vocal capacity of shattering glass and causing mini earthquakes) in solving musical capers. Together, they are the Masked Musicians.

The Llama Always Works

It wasn't the first time the Masked Musicians witnessed llamas falling from the sky. The phenomena happened every few months or so and usually when they least expected it.

"Cut it out, will you?" Lozenger hissed from behind a crate as the storage car rocked from side to side on the rails.

"How was I supposed to know they were transporting llamas *on* the train?" Llamaphilist retorted from within her barrel. Llama after llama leaped from the roof of the train and sprawled down the banks on either side of the tracks before running back up the slope to body slam the car where the supers were hiding. How they got onto the roof in the first place, she didn't even want to know.

"Make them stop!" Lozenger squeaked, his face blanching. "I'm getting train sick!"

"I'll see what I can do, but you know how temperamental llamas can be." Squeezing her eyes shut, Llamaphilist concentrated on establishing a mental link with the crazed body slammers outside. Silence settled on the car – apart from the groaning of wheels rising and slamming on rails and the muted thudding of llamas, that is. She huffed in frustration. She wasn't getting anywhere with the stubborn creatures. Cautiously peering both ways, she crawled out from her hiding spot and tiptoed to the nearest window. The latch unclasped easily and she hoisted it open.

"Here now, stop that!" she commanded the herd. Immediately the thumping and thudding ceased as all llama eyes focused on her. She waved her hand, "Go find some grass to munch. Be normal. Shoo!" Without much of a protest, the llamas dispersed, apparently more than happy to stop bruising their fluffy bodies in exchange for some peaceful grazing.

"Next time I suggest a distraction, I don't mean llamas, okay?" Lozenger stood up from behind the crate and dusted himself off. "I almost caused a tremor with that yell! That really would have gotten attention."

Llamaphilist made a face, "Well excuse me, Mr. Loud-Mouth. You know I can't stop them from hearing llamatic thoughts when they're that close."

Lozenger snickered. "Llamatic? Really?"

Llamaphilist shoved the window closed. "Let's get back to the task at hand, shall we?"

"Oh, yeah. We have about, what, ten minutes before the train takes off to rescue our captive?"

"More if they discover the llamas are missing," Llamaphilist commented, casting an eye on the couple of llamas still milling about in confusion on top of the boxcar.

"Maybe that wasn't such a bad idea after all," Lozenger conceded.

"I told you. The llama always works."

"Not always," he corrected. "Sometimes."

Llamaphilist narrowed her eyes. "Always," she insisted. "Now, are we going to rescue the contra-bass flute or not?"

"Lead the way, boss."

Heading toward the door, Llamaphilist yanked it open and stuck her head out. The conductor and a few brakemen ran along the slopes, apparently at a loss as to how to corral the rogue llamas. She suppressed the instinctual desire to offer her services there and focused on balancing across the couplings to the boxcar where the contra-bass flute hopefully was. It had better be there, considering the Masked Musicians already meticulously searched through all the other storage cars on this train.

"Why did Rutherford have to smuggle it in on a train?" Lozenger complained, his arms lifting from his sides as he carefully placed his feet in the same order as Llamaphilist's steps across the metal links.

"Because if it went by plane, TSA would have a hey-day with it in security, and a train is much more reliable than a moving truck when it comes to pricey cargo." Llamaphilist jumped onto the train car and shouldered open the door.

Lozenger hopped off the couplings after her. "What does he want with a contra-bass flute anyway? Those things are so awkward looking. Why not steal a baritone sax or a bass trombone?"

"Because they're rare. There's only a handful in the world, you know. Rutherford would get a fortune on the Black Key Market to fund his next evil performance. Now, let's start looking. A train only delays so long."

Thankfully, this boxcar didn't have as many smaller crates, trunks, and parcels to wade through as the previous cars. After some minor digging and grunting and groaning, Lozenger tugged a bulging bundle wrapped in burlap from between two steamer trunks.

"Hey, Llama, is this it?"

Llamaphilist poked her head above the trunk she'd just forced open and squealed with glee.

"Yes! That looks about right." Dropping the lid, she scrambled over to examine the mysterious parcel. Untying the rope, she looped it over her shoulder and peeled off the burlap. Underneath the burlap peeked a black instrument case. In that case gleamed a contra-bass flute.

Then the train rumbled to life.

"Quick, grab the other handle and let's go!" Llamaphilist shouted. Together, the Masked Musicians waddled out of the car with the case banging against their shins. Some careful maneuvering, a little bit of fiddling, and they safely had the flute off the train and resting on the ground. Lozenger lifted a hand over his eyes to squint in the direction of town.

"How are we going to transport this to headquarters?" He turned back to his partner when there was no reply. His jaw dropped. Llamaphilist was already securing the instrument case onto the backs of two llamas with the rope.

"No. No way." Lozenger backed up, waving his hands. "I am not walking with those smelly llamas all the way back."

"Got any better ideas?" Llamaphilist huffed as she tightened the rope under the belly of the second llama. "It's not like you can carry it on the winds of your resonant voice, and I'm not carrying it all the way into town myself."

Lozenger crossed his arms over his chest and pouted.

"Admit it," Llamaphilist goaded, a slow grin spreading across her face.

"Admit what?"

"Come on, you know what I'm talking about."

"The llama always works," Lozenger sighed in defeat.

S.O.S.
by Stephen J. Mitchell

Name of female superhero: SOS

Name of human alter ego, if different: Sabrina Olivia Strauss

Superhero appearance (hair, eyes, body type, etc.): She has long, golden blonde hair and a mask that whites out her eyes.

Human alter ego appearance (if she has an alter ego): She has short hair and wears glasses. Her left eye (green) and right eye (blue) are different colors. She loves wearing dresses.

Costume: She wears a white gymnast outfit with leggings, along with red boots, gloves, a mask and a short red cape that goes to the middle of her back. The letters SOS are interlocking down the middle of her chest where the bottom loop of the top 'S' joins with the top loop of the bottom 'S' to form an 'O' in the middle. She also has a belt with pouches to carry things (i.e. cell phone).

Personality: She is kind and caring with a dash of silliness.

Brief description of how she got her powers: She was born with special powers that have slowly gotten stronger over the years.

Powers: She has super-strength, super-speed and an indestructible body.

Anything else important: She has taken gymnastics since she was five years old. She has two moms; she was adopted and doesn't know who her real parents are. She loves painting, and she is an excellent student in school.

Double Jeopardy

You know what is worse than fighting crime?

Seventh grade drama.

No, not a class that teaches acting skills, I'm talking about the drama that happens between classes. I have enough problems fighting crime, but having to deal with problems at school makes a girl's life twice as hard! This year, my friend Sherry decided she was going to try out for the school spirit squad. When she asked me if she should, I squealed! Of course she should tryout, she's got more school spirit in her little pinky than an entire student body!

The problem is, she was turned down because of her size. I felt awful, like I should've seen it coming. I guess sometimes I get fooled by my own desire to see the good in people; I forget not everyone thinks the same as me. They wouldn't even let her tryout. You see, Sherry gets picked on because of her weight. That really bothers me. I don't understand why kids have to be so cruel.

"Tell me about it."

"Hush, the cops will be here any minute. Now just sit still and listen to my story."

Sheesh! Of all the bad guys, why did I have to catch the opinionated one?

Anyways, the kids at school say mean things about my friend's size. It makes me sad. I understand that some kids are overweight, some have acne or even just perpetual bad hair days. But none of those things matter when it comes to who they are on the inside.

In spite of her size, she's quite athletic. She's really good at soccer! But none of those kids would ever know because they don't even give her a chance. I've got to find a way to get those kids to see that Sherry would be a perfect fit for the spirit squad.

Unfortunately, changing a kid's mind isn't easy.

"Hey, are you sure those cops are coming? I've learned my lesson. Howz about you let me go and we let bygones be bygones, huh?"

"Are you not listening? I said, '*changing a kids' mind isn't easy.*'"

The thing about Sherry is her positive attitude never goes away. She's so brave!

When I asked my mom's about it, after my homework was done and before hitting the streets –

"And me!"

"Shush!"

Mama Nader says that people who live in glass houses shouldn't throw stones. Everyone has flaws, and for some people those flaws lie within their own heart. Maybe they try hiding their flaws by directing everyone's attention somewhere else? Those are the people who need to be loved the most, I guess. If they knew what it was like to be loved, perhaps they would want to share that feeling with someone else.

Both my mom's think I'm brave for fighting crime, but the kind of bravery Sherry has far outweighs my own. I don't know if I could come to school with a smile each day, knowing I'm going to get insulted for how I look. And believe me, I do! Being a girl with two-different colored eyes definitely attracts a lot of attention.

Her smile shines through the insults. And if Sherry can do that, maybe the girls at school use their insults to hide their own hurt.

"I wish someone loved me; I never knew my mom."

"And maybe that's what led you to a life of crime. Without a caring family, maybe you looked elsewhere for acceptance. Hence, your membership with the 'Booster Gang'."

"You tink maybe I could find a better family? One where I don't hafta steal cars no more?"

"With a little love and support, I don't see why not! A family should accept you for who you are, not what you appear to be."

And that's when it hit me! I'll start my own spirit squad that accepts anyone and everyone. I mean, with my art and Sherry's spirit, we can make some awesome signs to hang up in the halls. Plus, our squad won't be about appearances, it'll be about people coming together for a common cause. And whether you're big, little, socially awkward, handicapped or whatever – we'll be the best spirit squad ever, because what we'll support is togetherness!

"Dat's beautiful."

"Are you crying?"

"Only because you poked me in the eye earlier."

"Well, you tried to hit a twelve year old girl with a crowbar; what'd you expect?"

As the police arrived to collect the car thief, I quickly exited the scene. Getting caught up in answering questions could keep me past my curfew, and I had a lot of work ahead of me tomorrow. I need my sleep, and Mama Karen needs her sidekick home in time to help with the Double Jeopardy round.

Dark Sarah
by Kevin Hammond

Name of female villain: Dark Sarah

Name of human alter-ego, if different: Sarah

Super-villain appearance (hair, eyes, body type, etc.): She has red hair and pale skin.

Human alter ego appearance (if she has an alter ego): She has red hair and pale skin, and looks no different than she does when she is using her powers.

Costume: She wears normal, everyday clothing.

Personality: She is dark and brooding.

Brief description of how she got her powers: She gained her powers by the force of a little weirdo who judged her personality

Powers: She has the power to take life and the ability to manipulate dark power.

Anything else important: She has a super hero opposite who uses light for the power of good.

Light and Dark

Inglorious Mondays suck forever. Sarah scrawled the lipstick words on the bathroom mirror. Her boyfriend, Freddy, left his cell open on the kitchen counter. He didn't even care about being caught.

Combing her long red mane into some semblance of order, she snapped up his bottle of insulin, throwing it in the laundry chute.

Outside, the night was chilly and the sky was dark like a big creepy cape on the back of Dracula. The streets were deathly quiet. She thought about the other girl, Jenny. Like the song, Jenny painted a picture; it was a picture of desperation. She was all glee-club happy and struggling in New York City as a starving artist, only her rich parents paid the bills. She had slashed Freddy's tires and bought him his favorite cologne to keep him. At 5ft 8in with long red hair and creamy white skin, Sarah was a better catch; everyone knew it. Why couldn't Freddy let the creep go?

Sarah's musing was shattered when she realized she almost walked into some little guy who'd popped out of thin air. "Excuse me," she said, trying to maneuver around him but he held up a hand. In the dim light, she could see he was painted up in black and white, bald, and dressed like a monk. Before her, he placed a tiny music box on the ground. He wound the crank around a few times to sound the first few tinkling notes of *'Pop Goes the Weasel.'* In response, Sarah pulled out her can of mace. "Move it, freak!" she barked.

But the little man held his ground and pouted in a sad face, using his fingers to wipe fake tears from his eyes. Then he snarled, a fierce expression full of fangs and hatred. Black smoke billowed from his mouth and his hands, enveloping Sarah. It burned her skin wherever it touched, and she had not the will to utter a scream, such was the fear.

Sarah ground her eyes shut amid the tears.

When she opened them again, he and his music box were gone. In the air, she could hear the bouncy melody of his music, so she followed it into an alley. Stopping with a start, she saw a robber taking aim at an old couple. The old man refused to give up his dignity along with his wallet. So the love of his life took the bullet for him. Sarah watched, knowing it was a cruel lesson to accept. He handed over his wallet as he had nothing left in the world to care for.

She had done nothing to help. When the gunman took off, she walked to the old man who stood alone and desolate. His sad eyes beseeched her and the music jingled faster and faster – until she held out her hand and black tendrils snaked around the old man's neck to snap the life from his body.

The music stopped. And she understood. The man could never be happy, and she had come to end the cruelty the world inflicted upon him. But the musical notes were tinkling again. She could hear them and see them floating in the air. She could see Freddy lying alone in bed, and he could never be happy with or without her. She understood it all. Sarah began the walk back to his apartment.

The power was growing within her as she walked. The world around her was fading from color to black and white. Dark shadows pressed out from under her feet and the stars above faded away. All color fled except for one place, in a small park off the main street.

In the park, Sarah could see the little weirdo. He was different for the other girl whom he had cornered. His was painted up like a clown and he performed a capering little dance before a girl who clapped her hands in delight. Disgusted, Sarah turned away from the scene. How many others would the freak capture and turn into whatever she was now? On the walk to Freddy's apartment, she knew she didn't care. The weirdo had his purpose and she had hers. It was of no matter.

Outside Freddy's apartment block, she held out her hand and the black venomous smoke billowed over the door lock. The door blasted open with a heavy crack, and the smoke carried her in with her feet hovering above the ground. Sarah enjoyed the full weight of her own power as she drifted toward his door. That door drifted open with a silent swish. Sarah stepped down, light and full of dark grace, to walk over the soft brown carpet of his home.

He was still asleep. He lay so peaceful in his bed; he would never know of the cruel mercy she was to bring down on him. "You will never be happy without me," she said with a sad smile. Black tendrils snaked out from her hands to caress the bed he lay on. They drifted up and over his sleeping form, poised to strike. It would take but a few seconds.

It was then that the bedroom window exploded into the room and another girl stood, daring and proud. Sarah glared at her with menace for toying with her prize. She was confident of her power and knew she could banish this creature who had so much color and light. The black tendrils circled around the girl who stood showing no fear. "My name is Hannah," she said. "And wherever there is darkness, there is also light."

The room exploded in a blinding haze of color, and Sarah was thrown from the window to land with a sickening crack on the pavement below. Fear stirred her to up and run with those words echoing in her mind – *'Wherever there is darkness there is also light.'*

Warrioress
By Rebecca Fyfe

Name of female superhero: Warrioress

Name of human alter ego, if different: Marie Eden

Superhero appearance (hair, eyes, body type, etc.): She looks like her everyday self, except for a small mask over her eyes.

Human alter ego appearance (if she has an alter ego): She's a mother and a wife. She is usually wearing jeans and a blouse, sometimes a long skirt. She has long strawberry-blonde hair and green eyes. She's in her late 30s and is slightly muscled but just a little bit rounded in appearance.

Costume: When she has time, she wears a mask, but she doesn't always have time to hide her identity. When she encounters someone while out with her husband, she just does whatever is needed without worrying about hiding her identity. When she is going after someone who has been hurting others, she prepares by putting on the mask first. She even has a short cape for those occasions.

Personality: She's sweet and outgoing. She's fiercely loyal to her husband and her children, as well as her friends. She feels protective of children and puts on the mask to go after villains who have been hurting women or children.

Brief description of how she got her powers: She was always a little bit stronger than anyone expected or was normal, and just a tiny bit faster, but not in a way that was overly noticeable to others. She trained from a young age in martial arts, and when a friend's teenage daughter was beaten and left for dead, she decided to put some fear into the perpetrator of the crime before he ever tried doing something like that again. That's when her identity as the Warrioress was born.

Powers: She has strength equal to two very strong men, and she can move very quickly, more quickly than an average person or even someone who trains for races. She is trained in martial arts.

Anything else important: Her husband knows about her secret identity and its purpose, and he is very supportive. Her children do not know about her secret identity or that she fights criminals. She wants to keep them in the dark about it in an attempt to keep them safe.

An Unexpected Battle

Marie walked beside her husband in the crisp night air. The movie had been okay but nothing to get excited about. It had been enjoyable to get out away from the children for a few hours though. Dinner and a movie with her husband had been a welcome break. James gently slipped his hand over hers. It was only a short walk home. They'd given up their car many years ago and never regretted it once. Most places were within walking distance from them anyway.

The clouds moved and the light glow of light from the moon disappeared as they started walking across a field, just up the road from their house. A shadow moved in front of them, and Marie was startled when she felt James' hand grip hers tighter and pull her up short. She looked up and saw a man standing in front of them. He was almost as tall as her husband and was built like a linebacker. It was difficult to distinguish his features in the dark, but there was enough light from the nearby streetlights to glint off the knife he held in his right hand.

"Hand over your wallets and jewelry, and no one will get hurt!"

James held up his hand in a placating gesture. "Okay, we'll do what you say. You don't need the knife." He reached into his back pocket for his wallet.

In the next moment, the thug had hit James over the head, knocking him forcefully to the ground. Stunned, Marie could only think that he must have thought James was reaching for a weapon.

"Why did you do that?" Marie surprised herself by yelling at the thug. "He was just getting his wallet out like you asked!"

"I'm the one with the weapon here, so shut up!"

Marie could tell this guy was not the brightest guy they'd ever encountered, but he was right in that he was the one with the weapon. He was also nervous and violent, and Marie wasn't convinced that handing over their possessions would earn them any safety from him.

She took a step toward James as he got to his knees and tried to stand up but was brought up short by the thug snarling, "Stay where you are!"

"I will not! My husband is hurt and I'm going to help him."

The thug moved towards her, moving faster than she had thought him capable and, within a blink of her eyes, he was standing behind her holding the knife to her throat. By then, James was standing and growled out, "Let her go!"

"Stay back or I'll cut her!" the thug yelled.

Marie was getting really tired of all of this posturing by the thug and she decided that enough was enough. This guy was violent and dangerous, and he was threatening both her and her husband. If she didn't do anything, one of them might not make it home alive to see their children again. She would not be threatened by this moron any longer. Besides, how many others had he hurt and threatened before getting to them? She clasped her hands together and swung her elbow back with as much power as she could put into it, hitting him in the middle of his gut while stomping hard on his right foot at the same time.

The thug made a muffled "oof" sound as he bent forward, his knife nicked Marie's throat slightly as he pulled his hands into his stomach and let go of her. While he was still doubled over, Marie spun around and kicked him in the face. She heard a crunching sound as her foot made contact with his nose.

James was about to move in to help, but realized that Marie was handling the situation quite well on her own. He stopped for a brief moment, experiencing a swelling of pride in her. He watched her kick and pummel with the grace of a ballerina in her movements, coupled with the force and power of an avenging angel. She was stunning in her ferocity. He'd always known she had it in her. She was normally easy-going, funny and sweet, but he'd seen the fierceness in her eyes whenever she thought her children were threatened. He'd seen before how fierce and courageous she could be, his own beautiful warrior princess, when given the right circumstances.

But really, he was beginning to feel sorry for the idiot who had decided to threaten the two of them. He was laying on the ground now, blood pouring from his nose, holding his hands over his head as he curled into a defensive ball. James supposed he should take pity on the criminal and call the police before Marie did any more damage to him. That was always his job when she took out one of these creeps.

Sand Scorpion
by Michael Norwitz

Name of female superhero: The Sand Scorpion

Name of human alter ego, if different: Elisabeth Sanford

Superhero appearance (hair, eyes, body type, etc.): She is a young woman in her mid-twenties, with golden hair and eyes and a voluptuous figure.

Human alter ego appearance (if she has an alter ego): Elisabeth Sanford has made a reputation for herself as a socialite and can frequently be found at the 'hot spots' wearing an evening gown.

Costume: The Sand Scorpion cuts a fine figure in her sleeveless, body-hugging, yellow jumpsuit. A red bandanna with eye-slits covers the upper half of her face. Blonde hair falls around her shoulders from beneath the bandanna. A red scarf wraps itself around her waist and is tied-off to one side, with a strange looking pistol tucked into it. Both the collar and shorts of her jumpsuit are purple. Above the left breast is the embroidered image of a scorpion.

Personality: She has a playful manner and enjoys nights out on the town but has also witnessed the brutality of crime and takes it very seriously.

Brief description of how she got her powers: The daughter of a District Attorney, she used her first-hand knowledge of war criminals and deductive reasoning skills to aid the police.

Powers: Sand Scorpion was known for her combination of athletic maneuvers and detective skills.

Anything else important: The heroine was active in the United States in the 1940s.

Gluey Gustave

The blonde woman opens her mouth and exhales, watching in the dark as her breath forms a cloud of steam. That makes it officially cold, she decides, and pulls her jacket closer about herself. She turns her eyes from her binoculars, rubbing them as she yawns and nestles down into the parka she had thrown over her jumpsuit. She shifts atop the picnic blanket that lay over the roof of the building across the street from the restaurant, Il Maiale Viola, which she was observing. "I must have drifted off," she thinks to herself.

She hunches her shoulders slightly and settles down to watch once more. "I think my boy just drove up." She observes the garishly dressed man who lumbers from his car and into the alley behind the restaurant.

She swings down the nearby fire escape, moving quickly and silently. Arriving at the alleyway, she shouts, "Halt! You're under arrest!"

"Mon dieu!" exclaims a man dressed in an ugly green jumpsuit. He is wearing a purple beret and matching goggles, as well as purple gloves and boots. He is carrying a pail of glue, which is connected via a flexible hose to a gun. He looks the woman up and down. "What a fine femme 'az come to greet zee eyes of Gluey Gustave!"

'*Oh swell*,' she thinks. "I'm the Sand Scorpion, and I'm taking you in for, ah, grease theft." She reflects back on Giuseppe, the maître' d of Il Maiale Viola, and his account of how grease thieves were prowling about restaurants after hours, stealing gallons of the stuff and selling it to rendering plants for use as soap, cattle feed, cosmetics and explosives. The rendering companies paid up to five cents a pound for used grease, picking up sealed containers left outside by restaurants. But thieves were arriving first, carting it off and selling it on the sly for three cents a pound. The restaurant had been getting hit twice a week for the past two months, and losing as much as one hundred pounds, four or five times a month.

She runs at Gluey Gustave and tries to grab his gun, but gets glooped before she can do so. "Ew," she says, and readies her own gun, which fires her dart-like 'scorpion's stings.'

"That's enough," she says. Gluey Gustave moves surprisingly quickly, his glue sealing her weapon before it is able to discharge. A third blast from the glue gun secures her to the ground of the alley.

She sighs and peers at the villain. "Oh, I suppose you're too clever for us girls, um, Monsieur Gustav."

Gluey Gustave smiles, fingers twirling his mustache debonairly. "Few women can reseest zee charms of zee man with zee pail of glue."

She smiles back. "So I see. You know, maybe I should rethink my strategy here. I can certainly see the advantages of being conjoined in a union with as brilliant a criminal as yourself."

Gluey Gustave swaggers over to her, his eyes running up and down her voluptuous form. "So tell me more," he whispers, running his hands along her sides.

"Well," she whispers into his ear, as she reaches down to grab his glue pail and upend it into his face, "you really are an idiot."

"Aargh," he ejaculates as he staggers backwards. "Swing batta!" she shouts, and as her opponent stumbles within reach, she swings the butt of her gun into his head, knocking him out.

She watches him fall to the ground.

'*How can I get myself free?*' she thinks to herself, '*I can't even let go of this gun.*'

She sighs and peers at the unconscious criminal again. '*If he starts to wake up, I'll just hit him in the head again. That will make me feel better, at least, until I think of something.*'

Divine Light
by Robert Fyfe

Name of female superhero: Divine Light

Name of human alter ego, if different: Angelica Lumos

Superhero appearance (hair, eyes, body type, etc.): She is petite, with straight, dark hair, and wears white. She has wings.

Human alter ego appearance (if she has an alter ego): She wears normal, human, young-woman attire, and her wings are hidden from view.

Costume: She wears a white outfit and always carries her sword. Her sword is a piece of jewellery that wraps around her hand and wrist and transforms into a blade when she needs it.

Personality: She is sarcastic, witty, strong in character and purpose, fearless and self-reliant.

Brief description of how she got her powers: She was an angel born into a human world, but she was mostly unaware of her powers until, when she was a teenager, the angel Gabriel fully unleashed her powers.

Powers: She is the Vengeance of God and wields the Sword of God. She has super strength and the ability to smite. She can fly, has perfect agility and the power of an angel. She glows and has the power of invisibility to hide from humans and more.

Anything else important: She has a rough life before finding out her purpose, but came through it without letting her spirit be darkened. She doesn't choose her targets. She is sent after only the ones who are past redemption.

The First Reaping

Her heart was pounding and, again, Divine questioned if this was just all a sick joke. She faced her prey who now stood staring back at Divine. A mixture of terror, confusion and panic was evident as the woman backed up to the face behind her, the rattle of the metal mesh link sounded loud as it defied the woman's attempt to press through it to get away from – From what? Divine wondered what this vile creature thought she was now looking at. She thought about the clothes she had chosen as her reaper outfit, and suddenly jeans and a dark polo neck jumper didn't really seem appropriate attire for taking the life of another, even one so wretched as this piece of scum.

Divine realised that the woman's demeanour had change. She had obviously taken Divine's look of curiosity as a sign of confusion or weakness, something that she could manipulate to gain the upper hand.

The woman took a step away from the fence, "What are you?"

Divine was a little taken aback by this question. Weren't the big white wings and astral light enough clues?

"Do you think a halo will help you get it?" she asked, a little annoyed at herself for not thinking through her appearance and what her responses to questions about the fact she was an angel might be.

"But you can't exist! You can't!" It was obvious that the woman was still troubled by the vision before her, questioning herself, trying to reason away what would be an affront to everything she had let herself become. It was also evident that the dark, cruel, scheming and evil part of her soul hadn't gone away, for her eyes were searching every inch of this thing in front of her for something.

Divine had noticed this and had quite expected it. She remembered how the bullies were always looking for trouble, making sure that she had not been carrying anything that could be used against them; they had learned that very quickly at the orphanage, and here was the same look again, the one looking for trouble. *Well, look carefully*, she thought, *look, no knife, no gun, no baseball bat, no fork, not even a biro*. Divine could see the woman was evaluating her. Small, petite, girl, yes, but the wings, they were imposing and definitely cool in relation to impact.

The woman took another step forward, her strength of resolve now returning since the initial shock was wearing off. "Whatever you are, *whoever* you are, you need to leave."

Divine admitted to herself that she wasn't sure what she was going to do. She wasn't even sure that she could go through with the whole smiting thing anyway, but here she was, standing in the way of escape for this woman. She looked like she hadn't eaten for days, with dark rings round her eyes and a voice that was raspy from smoking whatever she had managed to scrape off the pavement. *I mean*, she thought to herself, *maybe this woman had been desperate, maybe she had been forced to do things that had just escalated into evilness*.

The woman took another step forward. "I'll give you one last chance to go, one chance to run, before I decide to do something you wouldn't like."

Divine took a step back, unsure of what she would do now.

The woman almost smiled with what she took to be hesitation, uncertainty, even fear, and took a larger, more forceful step forward. "I've hurt girls like you, you know?"

Okay, not feeling so sorry for her now.

"Killed little girlies like you."

Divine took a deep breath in and stood tall, crossing her arms over her chest.

"Eaten little girlies like you." Now the woman had convinced herself that she was stronger than this girl with wings. An evil smile now appeared on her face.

Divine thought of Terri, her friend who had run off from the home several years ago and had disappeared for a week before the police had found her, or had found *some* of her, just enough to be able to identify – most fed to the wild dogs in the barn. She realised that she had clenched her fists. No, that wouldn't do, wouldn't do at all.

The woman was slowly moving forward and slightly to Divine's right, not trying to get to a place where she could make a break for it if she needed to, but to head off any escape that Divine might try to make.

So even now, even faced with a messenger from God, this monster was calculating the kudos of the prize in front of her. Divine's eyes narrowed; now she understood. Now it was all starting to make sense. Her fingers on her left hand started to straighten, slowly, so as not to draw attention to her hand. First, her index finger, then her middle finger and on to the little finger - as each finger drew alongside its neighbor, the fine gold jewellery that adorned her fingers and hand slipped effortlessly together, the clips silent and yet strong. It was only once the procedure was complete that the streetlight sparkled like rain drops in the summer sun.

It was too late though, the woman had obviously passed into her evil self. She came at Divine, a scream of rage coming forth, drawn from the demons of hell itself, her rage pushing her on, her arms raised to shoulder height, her fingers reaching for Divine – reaching for her neck. Then it all came to a sudden halt, silent and still. Her arms were still raised, mouth open in mid yell, yet her eyes no longer looked at Divine; now they looked down, staring at her chest – at the arm that now protruded from it, the hand buried deep into the cavity that once held her beating heart, a heart that no longer beat, a heart that was being slowly pulled from her chest, not attached to anything, blood pouring from the clean cut arteries, falling onto her shoes. She looked at her killer and into the eyes of the angel, an angel that smiled at her.

"No more girlies for you now. Say 'hi' to Lucifer from me." Divine allowed the body to collapse onto the floor into a pile. She stared at the body, concerned that she had allowed herself to get emotionally involved in the kill. The thought of her friend's last moment at the hands of a monster such as this brought focus and the ability to complete the action without remorse.

She became aware of the light brightening behind her and knew without turning that Gabriel had appeared. "You said I shouldn't allow myself to make it personal; yet, in the end, I wanted to kill her and to do it quickly."

Gabriel's voice was calm and matter of fact, "I said we couldn't make killing a personal revenge, but I didn't say you couldn't enjoy it. In fact, it wouldn't be a good job if you found it difficult to do."

Divine looked absentmindedly at her hand, her weapon now disengaged and just the pretty hand jewellery it started out as. She looked at the heart, then let it drop down beside the body of the evil creature at her feet. Distractedly, she flicked her wrist to remove blood and, instantly, all traces of blood, organs, skin and heart, disappeared from her hand and clothes, as if her hand had never been buried elbow deep inside the chest and lungs of the monster.

She turned to face Gabriel, a question forming on her lips when she was interrupted by the sound of thunder, not from the sky but from the very ground they stood on. A vibration that slowly changed to a mini earthquake shook the ground beneath them, causing Divine to stretch her wings to support her balance.

"Ah! I forgot to tell you what happens now, didn't I?" Gabriel said with a glint in his eye.

SuperHERo Tales

Siren
by Rebecca Fyfe

Name of female superhero: Siren

Name of human alter ego, if different: Sienna Moon

Superhero appearance (hair, eyes, body type, etc.): She wears a mask and she magically turns her hair blue if anyone is watching her. She gains a full mermaid tail when in the ocean, along with a fin on her back, but she can manipulate her transformation into only having webbed hands or feet. She gains slight gills in her neck when under water, which are hard to see with her long hair in the way, and her ears are pointed.

Human alter ego appearance (if she has an alter ego): She has long, wavy, red hair with blonde highlights. She is petite and fit with light hazel eyes, freckles and pale skin.

Costume: She wears a mask and magically alters her hair color and eye color to blue when she needs to hide her identity.

Personality: She is stubborn and determined. She is outgoing and friendly but insecure. She is kind-hearted, but suspicious and somewhat cynical.

Brief description of how she got her powers: When she is in her early twenties, she goes to the beach one day for a swim, and she gets caught in a strong current. She gets thrown by an unusually powerful wave into some rocks and is knocked unconscious. When she wakes up, she is in a tranquil cove and she has a mermaid tail. There is a merman there who explains to her that she is a descendant of Poseidon. He explains to her that, as a "daughter of Poseidon" (as all of Poseidon's female descendants are known), she is having her powers awakened, and she is being called to work for Poseidon to save the oceans.

Powers: She has superhuman strength and agility. She can see in the dark. She can change her hair color or eye color at will. She can read emotions. She has a connection with other sea creatures. She can enchant with her singing, but it takes a while before it takes effect and her hold only lasts for three minutes after she stops singing. She can also call a large trident into her hand, seemingly from thin air.

Anything else important: Human pollution is killing the ocean, and once the ocean dies, the rest of the world will soon follow. She has to stop a powerful company in her home city from continuing to pollute the sea with chemicals which are killing off local sea life.

She has an ex-husband. He is a real jerk and the reason she finds it hard to trust. She has always felt the most at peace when she is sitting on the beach listening to the ocean's waves. She has always wanted to do something to help save the ocean and the creatures in it. She doesn't want these powers or the responsibility, but she knows that it is for an important cause.

The Guardian

Since she was a child, she had always loved coming to the beach and swimming. It was the place she always asked her parents to take her.

Now that she was a grown woman, with a job and bills to pay, she came here to escape. It was as if, with each stroke she made through the water, more of her worries would wash away.

She waded into the ocean and started swimming. She felt the sun-warmed water sliding past her skin and relaxed as she swam. This was her idea of Heaven.

Her Heaven didn't last long though. The water around her suddenly began to bubble and froth, startling Sienna from her relaxation. What was happening? She started to swim to where she could climb out of the water, but something from behind her shoved her just as she got to the shallow water again. A large wave picked her body up and tossed her into the air, then came crashing down on her. She fought to regain the surface, while the current held her under. Her chest felt tight. Pain blossomed behind her eyes and everything went black.

When Sienna opened her eyes again, she was still in a tranquil cove, but, aside from the pain she still suffered in her head, something else felt different. Her whole body felt different. She looked down at herself and gasped. She had scales! A mermaid tail! How? When? Her thoughts were racing, alternately telling herself she must be dreaming and then disagreeing with herself because it all felt much too real.

Movement to her left drew her eyes up. A merman was sitting on a large rock above the part of the bank she was laying against.

"Ah, I see you're awake now." His deep voice seemed to sing through her bones. "I'm sure you have questions, but if you'll listen for a few minutes, I'm sure I can answer them even before they are asked."

Her eyes were round saucers. She nodded, unable to find her voice. She kept thinking, *this has got to be a dream!*

"First of all, you are not dreaming." Sienna briefly wondered if he was reading her thoughts. "I am a merman, and you are now a mermaid. Well, technically, you've always been a mermaid; you just didn't have the tail to show for it."

He continued. "My name is Marcus, by the way. Shall I continue?" She nodded. "You are what is known as a 'daughter of Poseidon,' and your status as a daughter gives you certain gifts which he is able to call forth."

"Ahem," Sienna cleared her throat. "I know my parents, and my dad is definitely not Poseidon."

"No, he's not. The term 'daughter' in reference to Poseidon is more of a title. It means you are one of his descendants," he explained.

"What does any of that even mean? And can I get rid of the tail?" Sienna could feel her breathing speed up, and she concentrated on calming herself and breathing slower before she started to hyperventilate.

"You can choose to have legs instead, or you can choose an in-between form. You will be able to breathe under water now too. You will have other powers, but it's different for each daughter. There's no way to know which powers you will have until they show up."

"Well, uh, so, uh…" Sienna wasn't sure what to ask first. "Marcus? Who exactly are you? I mean, why are you here explaining things to me?"

"I'm your guardian. Every daughter has one. You have me."

"Oh. That's, uh, nice." Her first thought had to have been right; this was all just a dream. No way could any of this craziness be real.

"How do I get my legs back?" Sienna asked.

"Just concentrate on your legs. Think about them and you will transform back."

Sienna concentrated all of her thoughts on picturing her legs back in place instead of the scaly mermaid tail she now had. After some very intense tingling, like an electrical current running through her lower half, her tail transformed back to legs.

She started out of the water and Marcus followed. Sienna turned to Marcus, "Where are you going?"

"I told you. I'm your guardian. I'm coming with you. You need someone to help you through the changes and keep you from inadvertently revealing yourself to the world."

"Great. Just great," Sienna moaned.

Firestick
by Angelica Fyfe

Name of female superhero: Firestick (This is the name she is known as in the beginning. Later, people start calling her "Flicker.")

Name of human alter ego, if different: Jaseline Oranth

Superhero appearance (hair, eyes, body type, etc.): Jaseline's ethnic origins are not entirely known. She has tanned skin, and gentle freckles peppering her cheekbones and nose. She has an unusual pale birthmark just below her hairline, in the middle of her forehead, which glows bright white when she is powered-up. She has long, thick black curls, sapphire-blue eyes, a heart-shaped face, a petite frame, and she's about 5ft 3in tall. She has tiny wrists, and cute little feet but never likes to stay on her feet for long. When powered-up fully, she is coated in flames, deep red flames surrounding her coal-black hair, making them appear as fuel for the flames. Under abnormal circumstances, she has blue flames, the kind that could almost burn your retinas just by looking at them, which accentuate her eyes and make for a most foreboding persona. These are usually reserved for dire situations when her fire takes over and her conscious mind takes more of a backseat.

Human alter ego appearance (if she has an alter ego): Small and meek, Jaseline is an unassuming girl with bright eyes. She has the same physical features as above, but she covers her birthmark with make-up. She doesn't dress very outrageously and usually lets her hair fall in front of her face, when she's not tackling villains. She works as a waitress in a cute little café not far from her secret sanctum, and is often seen in her uniform – name badge, apron, and all.

Costume: Firestick likes her colour-code for apparel to be white, like magnesium heated up to a blinding whiteness. She also sees it as a kind of symbol of the purifying powers of fire, and as a symbol of her good, pure flames. She has a couple of outfits, but her usual villain-foiling attire is a leather armour-style outfit, with fitted trousers and a corset top. Skirts are just far too impractical for her taste. For other superheroine matters (such as ceremonies or award-giving), she also has a long, flowing white dress, made of soft, silky material that moves like the flames of a fire. She coats all her clothing – daytime work clothes or crime-fighting costume – with a special resin, extracted and modified from a rare plant located where she was born, which prevents them from burning up in her flames.

Personality: Quick-witted, bubbly, and spry, she believes in always doing the right thing. She likes to think that even the darkest of heart can be warmed up by a good soul, and if not, she will defend the innocent from those who would wish them harm. Her tendency to believe in everyone being inherently good, and only *choosing* to become bad, often leads her to make some poor judgement calls under pressure, and when others use her weakness against her and make her regret her mistakes, she comes back with a vengeance as fierce as the flames she bears. There's only enough oxygen for the world to stay warm, so any truly cold hearts she cannot abide by.

Brief description of how she got her powers: Jaseline was a lab rat. She didn't know it when she was younger, but the truth came out eventually. Born during an intense tribal ritual somewhere in the dense forests of South America, and taken to an isolated military base along the coast of California, Jaseline never knew her birth parents. She didn't know why they took her to the military camp, or what they did there, but something about her made the military scientists come for her in the first place. She managed to escape at a very young age, being picked up by social services at a later date. She accepts the fact that she was born already different, and she accepts that she has her powers for a reason. So it was this mysterious ritual birth and military intervention that lead to her unusual and unlikely abilities.

Powers: Firestick can fly; being a superhero, this is a pretty nifty skill to have. She can work the winds into shifting about to lift her where she needs to go, and this air-affinity also aids in her main power, for which she is so well known – her flames. She can produce various amounts of flames from her body, through her hands, her breath or her skin. She does not burn in it but can manipulate it and direct it as she likes – again, using the wind to guide it.

Anything else important: She was marked at birth with a symbol on her forehead, high up near her hairline, consisting of three commas (or "flames") swirling together, the outside of which forms a perfect circle. She has no notion of what it means or why it is there, but the mark is easy enough for her to conceal with a little bit of make-up and a loose-laying hairstyle.

Her main adversary, out of all her confrontations with evil, is the lady Eris, a militant woman with a coarse, deep voice. Eris has unusual beliefs and revels in causing chaos and disruption to the world. She works with a number of other overlords at the Facility, the military camp which Jaseline was brought to as an infant. There, they imprison and experiment on various "unique beings" like her. They use these powerful prisoners to do their bidding from time to time, whether they are willing or not. Jaseline has met a few of the others they keep there, and she pities them, though she has to defend against them. Eris is their keeper whenever they are brought out of the Facility to be utilised by the government order in whatever way the order chooses. She is the only one of them to be put out in the field, which is likely due to her immense skill in wreaking havoc.

Drowning

When she awoke, Jaseline had a breathing apparatus on and an intravenous drip steadily streaming fluids into her blood. She pulled the mask away from her face and sat up, her head swimming. She put a hand to her head, then froze. Eris was standing not two feet from the end of her bed, smiling.

"Good afternoon," the evil woman rasped in that hideously crude voice of hers.

Jaseline was up in seconds, pulling the needle from her hand and taking a fighting stance.

Eris laughed. "What good will that do? You can't harm me." She said, taking a step towards the frightened girl. "Go on, try it. Try to hurt me."

This confused her. Why would Eris be encouraging Jaseline to harm her? Not that she needed encouragement. The superheroine leapt out at Eris' face, aiming to burn it off with her flames.

But the flames did not come. Eris merely stepped aside to avoid the physical attack, and no flames lashed out at her.

Then Firestick fell, her neck roaring with pain and incapacitating her completely. She lifted her hands to it when the pain subsided, finding one of the Facility's collars. Panicking, Jaseline pulled at it, trying to yank it off of her, but this only caused her more pain. She howled in agony, then with shaking hands gingerly felt around the contraption, feeling spikes on the underside of the collar jabbing into her flesh.

A shadow passed over the girl on the floor clutching her neck, and she looked up to see Eris standing over her, smiling.

"Want to try again?" the villainous woman taunted light-heartedly.

Firestick's eyes burned with barely-suppressed fury, and Eris laughed and began to turn away from her.

In a flash, Jaseline was standing behind her, grabbing Eris by the shoulder and wrenching her backwards. The girl's fist was already clenched and flying for the woman's shocked face.

Stumbling slightly from the impact, Eris reeled away from the girl, shaking her head to clear it of the daze. She had barely a second to regain her senses before the little superheroine was underneath her, kicking out her legs. Eris toppled to the floor and watched as a foot came crashing towards her face. She rolled away from it just in time but remained on the floor. The girl, however, was already up and at the door, yanking it open.

A slow smile spread across Eris' face.

The superheroine was frozen in place, her hand still on the door. A silent moment passed before a tall, broad-shouldered man stepped in, his dark skin contrasting with the whiteness of the room.

His eyes were locked on Jaseline, and with each step he took, she retreated one.

Eris watched the girl back into the wall, and stood up, brushing herself off. "Enough." she said. At her words, the man moved his eyes off the girl, and, once released from his gaze, she collapsed to the floor, taking deep breaths as if she had been holding her breath the entire time. Which, Eris remembered, she would have; movement was made nearly impossible under Avery's cold stare.

It was odd that the girl *had* moved, especially with her powers bound. Eris made a mental note of this fact and put it to the side for now. Currently, she had matters to discuss.

"Well," she said, "now that we have that bit of ugly behaviour out of the way, let me make one thing abundantly clear:" Her pale eyes locked on the girl panting on the ground. "You are *mine* now. You can't escape – not even if you still had access to your powers and tried to *fly* away could you get out of here." She took a couple of slow steps towards the 'superheroine' and her mouth twitched up into a foul smile. "And while you're in here," she said in that deep, scratchy voice of hers, "I'm going to have some fun with you."

With that, Eris swept out of the room. Her dark cloak billowed out as she strode through the doorway, Avery in tow. The door clicked shut, leaving Jaseline alone on the floor, still sucking in air.

Eris' idea of 'fun' turned out to be Jaseline's worst nightmare. She stood on a thin podium, high up from the bottom of the massive dome she was in. Her feet and lower legs were locked in place with metal cases, the kind she could never burn through, even if she had access to her powers. The whole of the room was made of the stuff, save for the long window directly ahead of her, from where Eris and her consorts watched attentively.

Firestick could deal with being locked in place, unable to move – that was fine; it was the water that was slowly filling the dome from the floor upwards that was making her pulse race. She tried not to let her panic show, and instead glared across the dome to the viewing station, where Eris and her cronies watched her start to squirm.

The water was moving fast, and Jaseline couldn't help but look down at it, sloshing and crashing beneath her, coming closer. She ripped her gaze away from it, tried not to think of the water smothering her, but she couldn't seem to get her breathing back under control.

"You're afraid of *water*?" Zach called out to her from the viewing station microphone, disbelieving. His massive wings were folded tightly, held together against his back by some kind of locked harness.

"Shut *up*!" Jaseline called back through gritted teeth. Around her, waves splashed and rolled, the water level rising and becoming increasingly turbulent. She found it hard to come up with any decent retort as the water began to pool around her feet.

From his place next to Eris in the viewing room, Zach shifted uncomfortably on his feet. He didn't like what Eris was doing – he rarely ever did – but he needed to appear as if he did to gain her trust in order to finally get himself out of the Facility. He stopped fidgeting and watched the water rise around the girl, buffeting her.

Flames flickered out from her body. Zach blinked, confused, and watched the wind pick up in the dome. This time it was not Eris commanding the machines to direct the wind – it was Firestick.

The powers she had were pushing out from her, regardless of the barriers that Eris' collar imposed on her. Flames grew around her, roiling and twisting with the wind. They pushed past the waves battering against her, holding them at bay.

Zach turned to face Eris, who stood very still a few feet away from him. Her face betrayed nothing. "I thought you said she couldn't use her powers with that thing on," he said, frightened. The collars stopped *everyone* from using their abilities – he would know best of all.

Not getting a response, the winged boy turned back to watch Firestick battle the waves and defy logic but found he could no longer see her amidst the water and flames intermixing like some freaky firestorm.

The dome was almost completely filled with water now, and Zach almost felt as if he were at an aquarium, except for the blazing, steaming inferno at the centre of the tank – and the lack of fish, of course. Now that the water was above the glass window, Zachariel could see Firestick more clearly. However, what he saw tweaked at his heart (which he hadn't thought he still had anymore).

"She's panicking," Eris rasped with relish. A grin grew slowly on her face, making her appear even more sinister. "Excellent." She pushed a button and even more water was pumped into the dome.

Zach watched as the water pressed against the flames – and the flames went out.

His heart nearly jumped out of his body and abandoned him as he stood there and watched the girl he had fought with for years become swallowed up in the turbulent, rough water. Her hair billowed out like seaweed and partially obscured her face. Firestick's mouth opened as if to call for help, her eyes wide with fear. Water rushed in, and her mouth closed and stayed firmly shut for several long moments. Bubbles streamed out from her, and Eris hit a button to release the water.

But the water was going down too slowly.

She was thrashing now, stuck as she was by the metal gripping her legs as she struggled not to open her mouth and breathe in more water. Zachariel's heart pounded in his chest, aching to go and save his enemy from this cruel torture. *Eris wouldn't mean to kill her – she couldn't.* He glanced quickly at his leader. *Or would she?*

No, he decided, turning his gaze back to the girl in the centre of the receding water, she wouldn't. This was merely Eris' cruel method of testing the girl – and himself, judging from the way she kept her eyes on him from time to time.

Zach schooled his nerves into order and quieted his thundering heart. He would not show that he cared. Not that he *did* care, of course.

The winged boy could do nothing but calmly observe this entire heinous event as it drew to an end. Firestick (his troublesome Flameface) drew in her last breath, inhaling even more water into her struggling lungs. No more bubbles came out, and the superheroine's eyes closed as the leg-holders released and she floated in the centre.

Jaseline sputtered, coughing up icy water from *inside* her body. The world sharply regained focus as she was rolled onto her side by someone with big, warm hands. Her lungs burned, every breath feeling waterlogged and painful.

More coughing, more water. Then her body felt too tired to expel any more water, so she stopped sputtering to rest. She was rolled onto her back, and found she was staring up at an angel, silhouetted against the harsh light of the Facility compound. She blinked a few times, reasserting her scattered and exhausted brain. It was not an angel – it was Zach, and she was alive, not dead.

It took her brain a bit longer to process the rest. She looked around, at the water pooling around her face and lapping beside the platform they were all on; she had been drowned.

She turned back to Zach. She had died momentarily; he had brought her back to life.

Warrior
by Cecilia Clark

Name of female superhero: Warrior Woman

Superhero appearance (hair, eyes, body type, etc.): She has a strong, athletic body.

Human alter ego appearance (if she has an alter ego): She does not have a human alter ego.

Costume: She wears a skimpy leather bikini, studded arm bands and thigh-high leather boots.

Personality: She is aggressive, assertive and thoughtful.

Brief description of how she got her powers: She was drawn by a graphic artist and comes to life to teach him a few lessons about how warrior women really want to dress.

Anything else important: She cannot speak because the artist has not given her a voice. This is a story about the confusing messages about womanhood that both men and women are bombarded with in our society.

Warrior Women

Tim snarled at Rebecca.

"I'm sick of you nagging me about that kind of stuff. I'm drawing here! I don't want to think about that when I'm in the *zone*."

He rubbed his hair back from his forehead. Irritated and agitated, he directed his negative energies at her.

"What the heck are you wearing? You look like a potato sack. And can't you do something with your hair? How can I get perfect artwork if I am surrounded by ugly harridans? What does a bloke have to do to get some respect around here?"

He threw his graphite stub across the room, bouncing it off the wall near Rebecca's head. She ducked quickly, picked up the graphite, dropped it on his desk, placed his steaming coffee beside it and stood silently and patiently, waiting for him to calm down. The bright light through the office windows shone on his drawing desk.

"You agreed to do paperwork at this time; there are contracts to sign and your sister called to say that, if you haven't been to visit your mother, could you please send flowers for her birthday? Also the..."

"NO! Get out! Get out! I can't draw with all this crap in my ears."

She turned on her heel, picked up the empty coffee cups from the previous 24 hours, placed screwed-up paper balls in the bin and left the room. She returned with a pile of papers and laid them quietly on the desk beside his easel.

"If you wish your office staff to dress differently, you will need to write that in the job description. My resignation letter is in the pile of papers you have yet to look at. I suspect you will have few female applicants if they have to dress like your characters."

She walked out swiftly, without a backwards glance.

Tim's mouth dropped open as her comments sank in.

"Resign? Why the heck would you resign?" he yelled through the open doorway.

"Who else would take a frump like you anyway?" he yelled louder when he received no reply.

"Bah, who needs you? A hundred babes will be hammering at my door to work in a studio apartment with a famous artist."

He threw the stub of graphite again and shrugged.

"Now you, my beauty, you wouldn't whinge and nag about deadlines and birthdays or wear hideous clothes, would you?"

His bellow turned to crooning as he caressed the feminine shape on the paper in front of him. His graphite-greyed fingertip traced along her leg, following the naked line to the tight, barely visible shading of her bikini, on up the curve of her arched back to the tight leather bustier pushing up her bust to his lascivious eye.

"My beautiful warrior," he whispered as he slid his fingertip across her delicate chin and smudging some more shade in her loose flowing locks.

"You are the perfect woman – slender and beautiful, big eyes, big breasts, tiny waist, long, long legs and silent. I am completely in charge of what comes out of your mouth. How perfect you are."

Later that night, Tim woke abruptly, his throat constricted by a painful force against his larynx and his feet dangling above the floor. His sluggish brain struggled between the realisation that he was finding it difficult to breathe and the sensation of his pyjama pants sliding down his airborne legs. Dull green light widened his pupils as his brain registered details. Strong fingers held his throat at an even pressure, not quite enough to choke him but with a sure strength that let him know it was possible. The hand was attached to a muscled forearm and his eyes followed the length of arm to a bare shoulder, then a beautiful face – a face he recognised but could not place, hovered there, staring at him with angry eyes. He let his eyes drop to the delicate chin, the slender neck above a chest adorned with D-cup breasts in a skimpy leather bra. Tim's eyes widened in fear; he drew that bra, he knew every line of it. He looked back into the face of the woman holding him off the floor.

Her eyes were sparkling with anger, her lips as thin as the pencil line he had drawn them with. She looked him slowly up and down. He squirmed under her scrutiny and grabbed frantically for his striped pyjama waistband. He felt a glow of embarrassment as she lingered her gaze below his abdomen and sneered. She reached her free hand across and ran an exploring finger down his bare chest. His embarrassment deepened as she started a dry papery laugh and poked him sharply in the three hairs of his chest.

She dropped him abruptly at her feet and stood towering over him. He tried to crawl backwards, but she pulled the sword from the straps crossing her shoulders and stabbed it viciously straight between his legs, pinning the fabric of his pyjamas to the floor.

Tim gulped rapidly and noticed the sweat as it slid off his forehead, down his cheek and onto his neck. His armpits stung with fear. She pulled the sword from the floor and beckoned him with one beautifully manicured nail. He pushed himself up on his elbows and slowly uncoiled from the floor. She stepped back and he followed.

"Why won't you speak?" Tim squeaked.

She pinned him with a narrowed stare. One eyebrow rose in time to the curl of her lip and the wrinkling of her nose, she lifted a hand and opened her palm to reveal a stub of graphite. His own words came back to haunt him.

"I am completely in charge of what comes out of your mouth?"

He gulped and took the proffered drawing tool. As he touched it, an explosion of green iridescence engulfed him and he found himself standing next to a ghostly outline of an ordinary woman. He noticed she was careworn and tired, frumpy in clothing and hair, her shoulders rounded forward and her head bent. She reached for his hand and he began to shrink until she was twice his size. He recognised her.

"Mother?"

She looked at him with deep sorrow and leapt out the window, dragging him with her. His scream of terror stopped when he realised they were flying, not falling. Time and space fled past them, and he saw myriads of scene but never enough to make out details. He simply felt they were travelling backwards in time. She stopped in a village and pointed.

In the square, a woman stood with a mask on. The mask was metal and had been riveted shut over her head. There was a hole cut out for her nose and a slit for food and water. There was rust around the edge of her mouth. Again he heard his own words – *in charge of what comes out of your mouth* – but someone else was saying it. The woman wept. Other women looked frightened. A self-righteous man in a dark suit with short trousers, long knitted hose and a sharply starched collar with pleats, squared his shoulders, declaring to all in the town that no woman had a right to speak unless her husband gave her permission.

The scene faded and the sensation of flying stopped in another crowd and a bonfire. A woman in the bonfire was screeching in terror and pain. His words flowed back this time from a man in a black cassock declaring that *women who speak are the Devil's own handmaidens. Women who dabble in herbs must be burnt as witches.* The time sped up and the woman burned, followed by people and animals, sickening and dying for want of herbs while the frocked man waved symbols at them.

Tim and his mother's ghost flew again to a far place; the landscape changed and the air grew warmer. A tall African woman dressed in strings of bright beads stood silently with a spear. Tim could hear someone saying, "They are far more deadly than the men. The women warriors are preferred by the kings for their ferocity and loyalty. They perform with precision. They terrify me."

Tim turned his head to see a man in a French Colonial uniform before he faded and a new scene opened. Somehow he knew this was Sparta. Strong healthy women were sparring. "Women who would bear strong children needed to be strong," Tim could hear someone speaking. These women walked freely around their town, working, making decisions, bearing children, supporting their menfolk, unbound by constricting marriages of ownership. They moved through places where women held positions of power; he rode the waves with pirate queens who ruled huge empires full of devoted and loyal subjects. Tim was overwhelmed by sensations and suddenly pulled back to his room. His mother looked at him with utter sorrow, and tears fell from her face.

"Don't leave, Mother. I don't know what is happening."

He called out to her and reached for her hand as it dissipated.

The green glowing miasma surrounded him again, and, this time, a young girl stood in front of him. She was wearing dark rings of eye shadow and thick blood-red lipstick. Her tiny pleated skirt barely covered her hips and revealed lacy purple bikini pants. Her barely grown bust was pushed up in a parody of sexually appealing womanhood by a sparkly blue corset, and her midriff was adorned with a garish belly button ring of cheap rind stone and coated copper. Her look was completed by seven rings in her ears, her hair gelled into spikes, spiked bracelets, thigh high fishnet stockings and scarlet heeled boots. Tim blinked at her.

"Should you even be out at this time of night?"

He felt a bizarre sense of protectiveness toward this child-woman. She pursed her lips in a moue and shrugged her skinny shoulders. Grabbing his hand in her small lacy gloved fingers, she pulled him into the green swirls of fog. She flew with him to a wedding. The bride looked terrified and ten years old, the groom in his forties. Tim's shoulders started to tighten. He tried to pull his hand away from the girl's but her grip was glued to his.

"I don't want to be here," and he wasn't. He was in a jungle and a nine year old girl with the heavy swelling of pregnancy was being led by her eighteen year old sister to a clinic.

"No, no, I don't want to be here," Tim wailed, and he was in a brothel where tiny Asian girls and boys were waiting to be picked by fat old foreigners.

"No, no, no, this is wrong. This is not me. I want to go home." Tim arrived at another destination, a house in a town much like his own and there was a younger version of the girl holding his hand and an older version of himself. The girl had little ringlet curls and a night dress with tiny pink flowers and lace at the collar. She stood watching him draw another scantily clad comic book warrior. The TV screen in the background blared pop videos of women gyrating in skimpy shorts, with men dressed as pimps, singing about women as things to barter, calling them whores and owning no respect, no kindness, no love, just money. Past the window on bus sides moved posters about sexual arousal, ads flashed for toys talking about adult relationships, story books flipped open with subservient princesses. The child absorbed all the messages and turned to look at him. Tim felt a growing sense of dread. The girl had let his hand go and glided across the street. He watched helplessly as she leaned her tiny self into the window of a car and accepted a lift from a stranger.

"No, no, don't go there. No, it can be different. Please, don't get in the car. You don't have to do that," he called in despair as the scene faded. Tim felt sick. He, too, was being bombarded with images and ideas, and he was confused. He stood in his bedroom shivering in his pyjama bottoms. He hung his head in sorrow.

A rustling alerted him to her presence. The warrior woman stood in front of him as he lifted his head at the sound. She held out her hand, palm up, inviting him to take it. He looked at her face and she seemed less angry, more compassionate. He sighed and reached to take her hand and suddenly they were at a house he did not recognise. A young woman was packing boxes. She had red swollen eyes and a scrunched up tissue in her hand. It was Rebecca. He watched as she folded delicate things into paper and packed them in the removalist box, sealed the edges and marked each with a label and a coloured dot. Then she ticked her list on the clipboard.

"She is always efficient like that. Drives me crazy, but she sure keeps things working smoothly."

Time sped up and he watched in fast motion as she moved to another state, landed a new job in an advertising agency with good pay and a great working environment. She didn't dress any differently but she seemed to glow. Tim looked at her a little closer.

"She seems really happy. Good luck to her; she deserves a good job."

The scene changed and he watched himself sitting in a cold office. The lights were out, the heating off. A pile of unpaid bills with red urgent stamps littered the floor. He was slumped over his drawing desk amidst filthy cups and pizza boxes. He had put on weight and had a five day stubble. His shirt was sweat stained. There was nothing clean or pretty in the room and the pile of crumpled papers barely disguised the unwashed floor, the cobwebs and the general state of emptiness. His drawings were rolled up in a tatty cardboard box. The landlord was pounding on his door

"I don't need a bloody woman to keep my life on track, you know."

Tim felt a rush of anger and then a second thought pulled him up.

"I sure took everything she did for granted. She kept all that business side of my work running smoothly, and I wasn't prepared to pick up the pieces when she left. She was darn good at her job, and I let her leave. I just wanted to draw, and she made space for me to do that. It wasn't unreasonable to expect me to take the time once a day. I am such an idiot."

He slapped his forehead. He looked at the warrior woman beside him.

"I get it; you need more clothes, right?" She shook her head and took him to his desk in the studio. She pointed at the drawings of male super heroes and just plain heroes and tapped the armour. She mimed shivering. She mimed being hit by arrows and bullets. She was a good mime. She tapped the armour. She tapped pictures of jeans and rolled her eyes at the capes, miming getting her sword caught in it. Palms up, she looked at him waiting.

"Yeah, I see. You need freedom of movement to fight, but I like sexy. Is there really anything wrong with wanting to look at a sexy woman?"

She shook her head and pointed at the men and shrugged one shoulder, holding one hand palm up.

"So sexy guys are okay?" She shook her head from side to side miming big muscles, pointing at herself and then pretending to stick her fingers down her throat to puke, wrinkling her nose and slowly shaking her head from side to side.

"Muscled guys are not so attractive to girls?" She smiled and pointed to his heart, then gave him a thumbs up, then pointed to his head and gave a thumbs up.

"Oh, heart and brains, hey." She nodded.

"Can you truly tell me girls don't like muscles?" She put her hand out, palm down and rocked it side to side, tilting her head slightly and giving a half smile.

"Okay, so chicks..." She mimed a chicken and ran a forefinger across its throat.

"Oh-kay, babes…" She rocked a pretend baby back and forward in the crook of her arm and made an emphatic 'no' motion with her fingers.

"Okay then, women," she nodded, "like men who use their brains and heart and are okay with some muscle. And they like practical clothing on warrior women? Did I get that right?" She beamed a beautiful smile at him.

"Okay, I will try to make it right." She hugged him and her leather studded arm bands dug into his shoulder.

"Ow, okay, I'll get rid of the studs." She looked thoughtful and tapped her bracelets and gave a thumbs up.

"And leave the bracelets. Okay, anything else?"

She looked at him for a long silent minute, and he grinned.

"Give you back your voice?" Her eyes twinkled. She began to fade into the green light and, at the last moment, threw him something. He reached out and caught his phone.

There was a text message on the screen *'call Mum for her birthday then Rebecca to apologise and see if I can get her back. Note to self: maybe I should offer her a raise.'*

About the Authors & Illustrators

Lisa McLeod was born and raised in Silicon Valley, and despite being an avowed hater of cities, has not yet found a way to escape working for "the man" in order to build a cabin in the woods where she could ride horses, fish, grow her own food, and finish the dystopian Sci-Fi novel that she has been working on in her head for most of her adult life. Lisa is married to a computer science teacher/software game designer and they have a seven year old daughter, who shares her mother's love of animals and the country life, and a four year old son, who shares his mother's love of stories. Lisa has been trying to start blogging on the DailyKos.com under the username Resergent Voice where she hopes to vent some of the pent up frustration she feels about the corrupt plutocracy in America and its connections to problems in the educational system, climate change, de-unionization, and the hollowing out of the middle class. Dystopian, indeed.

*****

Rebecca Fyfe, an author with stories in several anthologies and collections, is a mother of seven children and, having lost over 145 lbs. of excess weight, blogs about health and fitness at SkinnyDreaming.com. She has always had a love for stories and books and graduated with a BA in English Literature and an AA in Child Development. She is a Californian who married an Englishman and now resides in Great Britain. Rebecca created and runs the Chapter Book Challenge (chapterbookchallenge.com) which runs every March, and, when not writing short stories or children's stories, she's busy creating urban fantasy novels, full of her own special blend of magic. She gets her inspiration from her five daughters and two sons. She is the founder of and editor at Melusine Muse Press (melusinemusepress.com) and owns several on-line gift shops, one of which can be found at moondusters.com. She blogs about books and writing at Imagine! Create! Write! (imaginecreatewrite.com). You can find her on Facebook (facebook.com/beckyfyfe), Twitter (@moonduster) and through her author blog at rebeccafyfe.com. You can find other books by her on her Amazon author page at amazon.com/Rebecca-Fyfe/e/B00EHAHGW4. Her illustrations can be found on pages 10, 37, 53, 73 and 100.

*****

Stephen J. Mitchell has been a lifelong fan of comic books and the superheroes who occupy them. He shares this passion with his three super-children. As a freelance writer he opines at his blog comic-book-nerd.com. He is actively involved with a writer's group as he continues to progress his powers of prose.

*****

Mark Dennion is a middle school English teacher who lives in New Jersey with his beautiful wife and lovely daughter in their small river cottage. He is also the author of the book series *The References*. *The References* is a superhero tale about a group of individuals who inherit reference book powers. The character "The Abacus" lives in the same universe as these superheroes. To find out more about Mark or *The References*, like us on Facebook at www.facebook.com/thereferences.

*****

Dee Harrison was born in Nottingham, England and brought up on the tales of Robin Hood and nearby Sherwood Forest. From this grew an abiding love for myths and legends. Dee studied medieval history at Nottingham University and decided to create her own myths. Thus the fantasy series, *The Firelord's Legacy*, was born. Dee is currently working on a new series featuring Junah Venmark, Master Mirrorsmith, and has written a special short story for

"Fusion," an anthology of fantasy and crime tales released by Breakwater Harbor Books. The collection won Best Anthology of 2014 in the Independent Book Awards hosted by eFestival of Words. Also published in 2014 was Dee's contribution "Closer" in the collection of stories "100 Worlds: Lightning-Quick SF and Fantasy Tales," edited by Milo James Fowler et al. Coming out in 2015 is "Nighteyes" through Astrid Press which features the story "Memory's Burden" by Dee. Dee has also had non-fiction essays on Medieval England published in Historical Journals. www.fantasywriter.co.uk

*****

Julia Stilchen is passionately driven by imagination and the exploration of new and original ideas for artistic expression - visually and in the art of storytelling. Her favorite genres are fantasy, futuristic and paranormal. She currently lives overseas with her husband and two children in Tokyo, Japan. Find out more about her on her website at julialelastilchen.com. Julia designed the cover for this anthology, as well as wrote one of the stories, including an illustration of it. Her illustration of her character Morpha Girl can be found on page 28.

*****

Tinika Ross is a novelist and poet from Southern New Jersey. She currently works in the insurance industry and does freelance writing. In her free time, Tinika can be found daydreaming or with her family and friends.

*****

Bron Rauk-Mitchell is an Aussie mum of four children and two furbabies. Bron has a BA, majoring in English and History, and has plans to further her studies in the near future. Bron tries to pack as much into life as possible, which is reflected by her many projects and interests. More about Bron's adventures can be found at http://essentialbronmitchell.blogspot.com.au and her other books she can be also be found on her Amazon author page at http://www.amazon.com/Bron-Rauk-Mitchell/e/B00ESEB5U8.

*****

Jo Hart lives in rural Australia with her husband and three young children. Her short stories appear in several anthologies and online publications. When she's not writing, she's a primary school teacher. If Jo could have any super power, she would love the power to clean her house with the snap of her fingers so she can spend more time writing. You can learn more about Jo and her writing at http://thegracefuldoe.wordpress.com. You can also find her on Facebook (facebook.com/JoHartAuthor) and also on Twitter at @gracefuldoe.

*****

Brian Norris studied musical composition under the tutelage of David Bucknam at Playwrights Horizons, where he wrote the book and lyrics for *The Snow Queen: The Musical, and Masquerade*. His new musical, *Immortally Yours*, was performed in concert form in Rochester, New York, in 2013. His memoir *The Hardest-Working Ballerina* was published in 2008, by Publish America. After a twenty year career as a dancer that took him all over the world, Brian is now teaching and choreographing. His illustration of Air-Heart can be found on page 48.

*****

Angelica Fyfe is an aspiring scientist with a BS degree in bio-veterinary science, and is learning all she can about animals, life, and science. In her spare time, she has accumulated an odd assortment of interests which have become her passions, including parkour, ninjutsu, belly-dance and, of course, creative writing. She is also a bit of a know-it-all when it comes to myths, magic, and monsters, and knows way too much about signs and symbols for her field of study (mitsudomoe, anyone?). If you can think of anyone more suited to fall through a fairy-hole, she'd love to meet them!

*****

Michael Tucker is an IT professional and a freelance artist from Chicago, Illinois. After serving in the Navy for six years and spending another year abroad, he received his BS in Management Information Systems (BSMIS) and also obtained certifications in Business Programming and Website Design. However, his first love was always art. After his fifteen-year career in IT as a Computer Security Administrator and Senior System Engineer, Michael decided it was time for a change. He now works from home, where he devotes time to writing, artwork and web design. He currently lives with his fiancée Lee, their dog Reggie, and their three cats Sox, Rory, and George. He can be contacted at the e-mail discombobul8d@gmail.com or at http://discombobul8d.deviantart.com.

*****

What toddler calls their toys "characters"? This young woman did, and she's dabbled with them ever since. **Mary MacFarlane** resides in Ontario, Canada with her darling husband and Pippy, her kitten. She occupies herself with crocheting, housekeeping, Bible studies, and working on her first novel. Should you wish to encourage, critique, or insult this beginner writer, her scribbles are located at www.frolickingfairies.blogspot.ca.

*****

After spending many years in his homeland of Scotland, East Kilbride to be exact, **Kevin Hammond** embarked on a journey across the ocean – destination: middle of nowhere Pennsylvania where he married and now lives with his wife and daughter. His current venture is a volume of books called "Magic, Fairy Tales, and Inter Dimensional Poking Devices". Volume one takes the reader on a magical and wacky story taking place in an alternate dimension where fairy tales just happen to be the main industry. Plenty of silliness abounds as the fairy tale economy faces collapse giving rise to the lollygaggers' movement. A wish is cast upon the wishing star for fate to be kind. Humor and mayhem ensue leading to a wide range of consequences that will unfold the sad story behind why the universe is how it is today. Volume two picks up where Volume one leaves off. Other titles available include the stand alone title "Loki's Hunt" available on Kindle or paperback through Amazon. You can also find Kev on his Amazon author page at http://www.amazon.com/Kevin-Hammond/e/B0072XMRGS or you can visit his Facebook page at http://www.facebook.com/pages/Magic-fairy-tales-and-inter-dimensional-poking-devices/372639562752883.

*****

Michael Norwitz lives in California with his wife and daughter and innumerable cats. He spends his time trying to be a helpful rather than an obstructionary bureaucrat, dancing, and is just now embarking on an attempted second career as a comics writer.
-

*****

Robert Fyfe is a father of seven children and husband to Rebecca Fyfe. He works in IT Business Management, and when he finds a spot of that elusive "spare time" people so often talk about, he does a bit of writing. You can find some of his art and digital photo-manipulation on Fairy Magic Photos at fairymagicphotography.com and on his page on Deviant Art at bfg.deviantart.com. His illustration of the character Siren can be found on page 87.

*****

Cecilia Clark is a multi-genre writer and illustrator with short stories in thirty anthologies, some published, some pending and flash fiction in e-zines, She sharpens her pen on 25-word or less competitions and wins every one she enters, gaining prizes from pianos to movie tickets. Cecilia also has art in the published works of other writers. Her first love is fairy tales, closely followed by SF, steam punk and fantasy, though her tastes are eclectic and unlimited. She has dabbled in writing horror and crime fiction and is currently working on several projects involving both. She can be found at the usual e-hangouts:

http://ceciliaaclark.blogspot.com.au,
http://www.pinterest.com/ceciliaaclark,
https://www.facebook.com/cecilia.clark.336 and
https://twitter.com/cc_lark.
She also has her works displayed on her Goodreads and Amazon author profiles.

*****

Kieron O'Gorman is an Illustrator working in Ottawa, Canada. He has worked as a freelance illustrator for role-playing games (RPG), board games, and has also worked as a penciller, inker, and colourist for comic books. His illustration credits include numerous RPG and board game titles: the Catalyst Game Labs Battletech sourcebook entitled "BattleTech Masters & Minions: The StarCorps;" various Savage Worlds products from Pinnacle Entertainment; Broken Ruler Games RPG system called "Killshot;" and illustrations for Sword's Edge Publishing RPG entitled "Centurion." He has supplied sequential art for some local comic publishers as well. You can find samples of Kieron's artwork online at: www.mayhemgraphics.com, or on his Facebook group: Kieron O'Gorman Illustration (https://www.facebook.com/kmanillustration). If you have inquires or would like to hire Kieron for illustration work you can reach him at kogorman@mayhemgraphics.com. "The Sand Scorpion" character and artwork within this anthology are his creation. His Sand Scorpion illustrations can be found on pages 78 and 117.

*****

Samuel Dixon is a recent graduate from the University of Lincoln, UK, and is an amateur music composer, guitarist and digital artist as well as being, most prominently, an expert tea brewer and drinker. He can be contacted on twitter at twitter.com/samd908. His illustrations of the characters Pegasus and Firestick can be found on pages 16, 92 and 116.

Editor:
Rebecca Fyfe

Foreword:
Lisa McLeod

Cover artist:
Julia Stilchen

Illustrators:
Rebecca Fyfe
Julia Stilchen
Samuel Dixon
Kieron O'Gormon
Brian Norris
Robert Fyfe

If you loved, "SuperHERo Tales: A Collection of Female Superhero Stories (Volume Two)," then you will also love "SuperHERo Tales: A Collection of Female Superhero Stories (Volume One)." The first volume includes more scenes from some of the same superheroes as in the second volume as well as several superheroes not found in volume two.

Buy your copy of volume one at
http://www.amazon.com/SuperHERo-Tales-Collection-Superhero-Stories/dp/1494218038

Printed in Great Britain
by Amazon